P9-DFT-433

THERE ARE TWO DIFFERENT OCCASIONS IN OUR lives that seem tailor-made for pausing to reflect, for taking stock, for looking back at how far we've come and ahead to the goals still to be attained: anniversaries and birthdays ending in zero. I have a few years yet until my next zero-ending birthday (the last was 30, if you're wondering), but in May 1993, LOVESWEPT will be ten years old, and I will have been a published writer for thirteen years.

I first signed with LOVESWEPT in June of 1983. By then I'd written eight or nine books, and I'd already had at least one book challenged (and subsequently changed) because the editor felt my ideas were too "risky" for the current market. Imagine my delight when I found, at LOVESWEPT, a total enthusiasm for my ideas and faith in my ability to make them work. Through the years, I have never, *ever* heard anyone at LOVESWEPT say, "You can't do that." No matter how wild the initial idea, the response was always, "Go for it."

Looking back ten years, I know without doubt that the editorial enthusiasm of those at LOVESWEPT, and their willingness to let me explore—to let me sail off in search of dragons, even if they *did* know the world was round—has made all the difference in my career. And looking ahead to the next ten years, I see some terrific possibilities . . . because I think there are still a few dragons left to be found.

Happy 10th Anniversary, LOVESWEPT!

Kay Hooper

WHAT ARE *LOVESWEPT* ROMANCES?

They are stories of true romance and touching emotion. We believe those two very important ingredients are constants in our highly sensual and very believable stories in the LOVESWEPT *line. Our goal is to give you, the reader, stories of consistently high quality that may sometimes make you laugh, sometimes make you cry, but are always fresh and creative and contain many delightful surprises within their pages.*

Most romance fans read an enormous number of books. Those they truly love, they keep. Others may be traded with friends and soon forgotten. We hope that each LOVESWEPT *romance will be a treasure—a "keeper." We will always try to publish*

LOVE STORIES YOU'LL NEVER FORGET
BY AUTHORS YOU'LL ALWAYS REMEMBER

The Editors

Loveswept ® 619

Men of Mysteries Past

THE TROUBLE
WITH JARED

KAY
HOOPER

BANTAM BOOKS

NEW YORK · TORONTO · LONDON · SYDNEY · AUCKLAND

THE TROUBLE WITH JARED

A Bantam Book / June 1993

*Grateful acknowledgment is made for permission to reprint
from "Reluctance," by Robert Frost, copyright © 1964,
Henry Holt and Company, Inc.*

*LOVESWEPT and the wave design are registered
trademarks of Bantam Books, a division of
Bantam Doubleday Dell Publishing Group, Inc.
Registered in U.S. Patent
and Trademark Office and elsewhere.*

*All rights reserved.
Copyright © 1993 by Kay Hooper.
Cover art copyright © 1993 by Joel Malmed.
No part of this book may be reproduced or transmitted
in any form or by any means, electronic or mechanical,
including photocopying, recording, or by any
information storage and retrieval system, without
permission in writing from the publisher.
For information address: Bantam Books.*

If you purchased this book without a cover you should be aware
that this book is stolen property. It was reported as "unsold and
destroyed" to the publisher, and neither the author nor the publisher
has received any payment for this "stripped book."

*If you would be interested in receiving protective vinyl
covers for your Loveswept books, please write to this address
for information:*

*Loveswept
Bantam Books
P.O. Box 985
Hicksville, NY 11802*

ISBN 0-553-44339-9

Published simultaneously in the United States and Canada

*Bantam Books are published by Bantam Books, a division of Bantam
Doubleday Dell Publishing Group, Inc. Its trademark, consisting of the
words "Bantam Books" and the portrayal of a rooster, is Registered
in U.S. Patent and Trademark Office and in other countries.
Marca Registrada. Bantam Books, 1540 Broadway, New York,
New York 10036.*

PRINTED IN THE UNITED STATES OF AMERICA

OPM   0 9 8 7 6 5 4 3 2 1

For Chase Allen Lancaster,
the nephew born while this book
was being written

Great things are done when men and mountains meet.
— WILLIAM BLAKE

Ah, when to the heart of man
Was it ever less than a treason
To go with the drift of things,
To yield with a grace to reason,
And bow and accept the end
Of a love or a season?

—ROBERT FROST
"Reluctance"

PROLOGUE

She moved through the frantic crowd at San Francisco International Airport, seemingly untouched and undisturbed by the commotion all around her. That was what caught his attention: not the gleaming dark hair or beautiful face, but the way she moved, graceful and deliberate, refusing to be hurried by the bustle surrounding her.

He remembered that about her.

He found himself almost swept into the swirls and eddies of the stream of people in the concourse, but struggled to get himself turned in the opposite direction. He had planned to leave today, but the plan changed the instant he saw her. Seeing her told him this was an opportunity that might never be repeated.

It was easy to follow her, easy to pick out the crisp white suit that didn't look as if she'd just spent many hours in the cramped seat of a jumbo jet. Easy to spot the dark hair swinging gently as she walked. He didn't worry about watching her too closely; even in the busy airport, there were so many people staring at her that she would never have been able to feel his gaze stronger than the others. And even if anyone else noticed his fixed stare, they wouldn't have found it surprising.

He had known in an instant why she must be in San Francisco. The Bannister collection, of course. The priceless hoard of fabulous gems, jewelry, and artworks was scheduled to go on exhibit in less than a month, which meant it would need to be readied for display after more than thirty years in storage.

Natural that they'd called her in. She was one of the world's top experts, after all. And her arrival, in the city, was as good as a shout proclaiming her business here. To those in the know, of course.

He knew. He followed her through the airport, his heart beating faster as he grasped the opportunity he'd been waiting for, his mind clear and cold as he began to plan.

ONE

The apartment building looked like any other expensive high rise in San Francisco, though it was newer than most. Built atop a hill in the modern section called Golden Gateway near the shore of San Francisco Bay, it rose thirty stories and boasted roomy luxury apartments with splendid views of the city and every possible convenience. And though it didn't look it, the building was also one of the most security conscious in the city.

Jared Chavalier reminded himself of that as he sat in his car watching the brisk activity of a dozen uniformed men unloading a moving van. Trained to be observant, he noted that none of the men appeared unusual, and certainly no one who didn't know would have guessed that all were armed.

After a few minutes, Jared got out of his car and blended into the flow of men carrying furniture, boxes, and crates into the lobby of the building. None of the men reacted overtly to his presence, except for one who offered a gruff, "Watch it, buddy," as Jared inadvertently got in the way of a sofa.

There was a desk in the lobby where two uniformed security guards were posted, and two more stood by the freight elevator intently eyeing each moving man as they and their burdens entered the car for the trip up. Jared paused by the desk to sign the security log; it was a mark of the high security here that he would have been asked to sign in even though all the guards knew who and what he was.

"Good morning, sir," one offered politely.

"Morning," Jared returned, signing his name and the apartment number he intended to visit.

The other guard, with another clipboard and an enigmatic little device on the desk before him, smiled and said respectfully, "If you wouldn't mind, sir?"

Jared reached into the inner pocket of his jacket and withdrew a plastic ID card, which he handed over silently. There was no name or picture on the card, but when the security guard passed it through the slot on the cryptic device before him, a quiet audio tone indicated that all the information magnetically encoded on the card was correct and approved, and was being noted in the computerized security system.

"Thank you, sir."

His card returned to him, Jared nodded to the

guards and continued past the desk to the regular elevators. Choosing a particular one and entering, he ignored the pad of numbers indicating the choice of floors and instead inserted his ID card into an almost invisible slot just above the backlit numbers. Obediently the doors closed and the elevator began rising toward the penthouse apartment.

When the doors opened again, Jared found himself in a spacious foyer. Across from the elevator, the double doors of the penthouse stood open, and as Jared stepped into the foyer a big, dark, hard-looking man came out to join him.

"Problems?" the man asked in a deep voice that was surprisingly soft.

"Not as far as I can see," Jared replied. "This is the last load, so everything should be up here within an hour. I've been watching, and I couldn't tell this building was surrounded by your security people, or that all the movers were out of the ordinary. If I hadn't known where Wolfe was, I wouldn't have seen him, and nobody else in the neighborhood seems to have taken any notice at all of what's going on."

Max Bannister smiled slightly. "So, do you feel a little better now about not using cops or an armored truck to move the collection?"

"I'm nervous as hell," Jared admitted dryly. "Given my druthers, I would have opted to keep the collection in the vault until it was time to move it to the museum. But—it looks like you've picked the best building in the city outside of a bank, another vault, or the museum. I just wish we'd been able to move it directly from storage to the museum."

In a patient tone, Max said, "It's going to take at least two or three weeks for the gemologist to get the collection reappraised and ready for display, even working very long hours. I wasn't about to ask anyone to spend that kind of time in a sterile vault with only armed guards for company. Here we can provide excellent security as well as a comfortable place to work and stay for the duration."

"I know, I know. I also know you're having a few more laser grids installed at the museum—on Storm's recommendation—which is why we can't take the collection directly there yet. But I don't have to like it."

Before Max could respond, the pleasantly camouflaged freight-elevator doors opened to deliver its load of men, crates, and furniture. The men didn't have to ask anyone where to put anything; each knew precisely where his burden went because he had been told ahead of time. Every detail required to make this transition as swift and secure as possible had been taken into account.

Watching as the priceless Bannister collection of fabulous gems and artworks was nonchalantly carted into the penthouse, its presence disguised in boxes and crates innocently labeled "knickknacks," "books," and "kitchen utensils," Jared said absently, "Speaking of the gemologist, I wish you'd let me run my own security check. We can't be too careful, you know."

"We've already run every possible check," Max replied patiently. "Morgan did a hell of a lot of research, and then ran her list of candidates through the FBI, your office at Interpol, Lloyd's of London, the International Foundation for Art Research, and about a dozen more organizations dealing with art, gems, gemologists—and everything else we could think of. The top five names we had were absolutely clean, their reputations utterly above reproach, and are acknowledged experts in their field."

Jared felt a sudden flicker of unease, but brushed it aside. "So, where's your expert?"

"She arrived a couple of hours ago, and Morgan brought her directly from the airport," Max said, turning to lead the way into the penthouse. "Come on, I want you to meet her."

As he followed, Jared's unease began to build toward alarm. But it was a big world, he reminded himself, and surely . . .

Max didn't seem to notice the silence. "Actually we were lucky to get her; she tops the list of world-renowned experts able to do the work we need. Her last job was doing some kind of work with a set of European crown jewels. She won't say what was involved because of security demands, but my sources tell me somebody tried to pull a switch and she caught it. It certainly sounds like she knows what she's doing. Along with all our security checks, Morgan spoke to several of her previous clients, and they had nothing but praise for her."

Jared's heart was beginning to beat with a slow, heavy rhythm that was almost painful. He barely noticed the spacious rooms, the lovely furniture being set in place, or the stunning views from every window—and not because he'd seen it all before. All his attention was fixed ahead of Max, toward the specially constructed room that was their destination. The relatively small central room was literally the apartment's safe, windowless and with specially reinforced walls. When closed up, it was so cunningly hidden that only a foot-by-foot measurement of the entire penthouse would hint at its existence.

The most recent load of crates and boxes had already been deposited in the room when Jared and Max arrived, so there was no one inside except for the expert gemologist Max had hired to ready his collection for public display.

In her late twenties, she was absurdly young to be a world-famous expert on anything. She was also incredibly beautiful, blessed with the kind of looks that would turn heads wherever she went. Gleaming hair that was very dark but with a hint of red fell straight and luxuriant to just below her shoulders. Her face was curiously both aloof and sensual, with delicate brows arching above eyes so dark they hid their secrets well, and lips so lush they were incredibly erotic. Tall, slender, and fine-boned, she had a splendid figure and dark coloring that were set off by the form-fitting white jacket and the short, white pleated skirt baring her exquisite legs to midthigh.

She was standing in profile when the two men came in, her attention focused on a velvet case she had just lifted from one of the many boxes stacked in the room. What she was looking at was the famous Bolling diamond, a seventy-five-karat canary set in a pendant of twenty-four-karat gold; the yellow stone glittered brilliantly even without the special lighting of a display case that would show it to advantage.

Max began speaking as soon as they came in. "Danica, there's someone I'd like you to meet. Since he'll be keeping an eye on the collection, you two will probably see quite a bit of each other during the coming weeks. Danica Gray, Jared Chavalier."

If her long, elegant fingers quivered a bit when Danica closed the case and set it back into its box before she turned to face them, only one of the men saw it.

"We've met," she said quietly.

Jared didn't go forward to shake her hand, or make any kind of move toward her at all. He stood with his hands in the pockets of his jacket—though he didn't remember jamming them in there—gazing past the clutter of boxes and crates at her still, distant expression, and he was furious to realize he couldn't force a word past the sudden tightness of his throat.

Before his silence became painfully conspicuous, they all heard Morgan West's harried voice calling from another room of the apartment. "Max! I need you. . . ."

"Since you two know each other, I'll leave you to talk," Max said, with a look at Jared that said much more. What he meant was that since Danica knew who Jared was, she might also know *what* he was—and might well wonder about his presence here. Max was leaving it up to Jared to decide how much to tell her.

Which was the least of Jared's concerns at the moment.

But Danica, who was nobody's idea of dumb, didn't give him much opportunity to avoid the subject until he had a chance to think it through. Standing with her fingers loosely linked together before her, dark, unreadable eyes fixed on his face, she asked, "Does Interpol loan out its officers to be private security agents, or are you moonlighting?"

"Neither." He knew his voice was too harsh, but it was taking all he had to force himself to speak in anything approaching a normal tone.

"Then how are you involved in this?" Her voice remained matter-of-fact.

"Maybe that's none of your business."

She wasn't noticeably put off by his terse statement. "And maybe it is. Since I'll be the person nearest it for the next few weeks, I think I deserve to know if the collection is more than the usual target for violence."

"Afraid of a little risk, Dani?" he asked mockingly.

She didn't react in any visible way to his taunting. "No. I'm simply interested. After all, I might want to raise my fee. Combat pay, I think it's called."

"There won't be any combat." The curt sound of his own voice bothered him. God, couldn't he at least pretend he wasn't affected by her sudden reappearance in his life? "I'm sure Max told you this is one of the most secure buildings in the city. And we've taken other precautions. With any luck at all, no one even knows the collection isn't still in the vault."

"Someone once told me that only a fool would trust his life to luck," she said.

Since he'd been the one to tell her, Jared could hardly contradict the words. "True enough. Let's just say that both you and the collection are as safe in this building as you can possibly be."

She hadn't moved since turning to face him, which didn't surprise Jared. A peculiarly still, composed woman, she had no nervous mannerisms whatsoever; it was another trait she was well-known for, and one which he found disconcertingly familiar.

He told himself to stop it, stop thinking about her, to concentrate on business.

"You haven't answered my original question," she said in the quiet, slightly husky voice that was also too familiar to him. "Are you here simply because Interpol expects the *Mysteries Past* exhibit to be a target for thieves?"

He was reluctant to lie to her outright, but since this was hardly the time to discuss a rather elaborate situation, he merely shrugged and said, "Yeah."

Danica looked at him steadily. "Then you will have to remain close to the collection. Do you want me to ask Mr. Bannister—Max—to find someone else to do this job?"

"Why would I?" He tried to sound indifferent, but to him he merely sounded truculent.

She blinked, but her face remained unreadable. "It was obviously an . . . unpleasant shock for you to find me here. I simply thought it might be easier—"

"I'm a professional, Dani," he said shortly. "I trust you are as well. I think we can both stand being in the same city for the next two or three weeks."

Danica inclined her head with a distant sort of politeness. "Very well."

Her detachment maddened him. Unable to leave the subject alone, he said, "After all, Max wants the best—and that's supposed to be you. You've been on top for a while now, so I hear. How did it feel to move into first place after Daniel died?"

She did react then to that abrupt question, though the reaction was almost imperceptible. Just a slight tightening of those lush lips, and a flash of emotion skimming the darkness of her eyes.

"What do you want me to say, Jared?"

That was what he'd wanted her to say, he realized. His name. He had wanted to hear her speak his name, even knowing the sound of it would open a floodgate of memories. And it did.

They were unnervingly bright and clear in his mind, the memories. How she had looked the first day he'd seen her, hair much longer than now, uncut since she'd taken her first toddler's steps, and her body more thin than slender with womanhood just beyond reach. Eyes fixed on his face with a wondering sort of absorption, as if nothing in the world had existed for her except him.

He'd been lost as quickly as that, obsessed with her as only a very young man or a very old man could be obsessed, intent on nothing except making certain she belonged to him.

Then the memories came quicker, washing over Jared in a tide, and he could hardly bear the weight of them. The nervous excitement in her eyes when she had felt desire for the first time. The hesitant touch of her delicate hands on his body. Her incredible mouth beneath his. A fragile spring of awakening sensuality that had become a tense summer of conflict and an autumn of growing hostility. A bitter tug of war. And, finally, in the coldness of winter, an end.

The memories were so terribly vivid. God, he could almost smell the stifling scent of the roses Daniel had filled his workshop with that day, a fragrance that even now made Jared sick to his stomach.

"Jared?" She was looking at him, not with fear but with an awareness that was almost primitive, instinctive, like a cornered creature's sudden knowledge of danger.

He realized dimly that he had taken a step toward her, that he had drawn his hands from his pockets and they were flexing as if in anticipation of some kind of violence. The sheer force of his emotions was almost numbing, unmanageable, and he knew with stark clarity that if he didn't walk away from her now, he would never be able to regain any kind of control.

Without another word to her, he turned and left the safe room, going out into the apartment with the deliberate stride of a man walking a mine field.

The moment Jared left the room, Danica sank down on an unopened crate behind her, trembling. She felt appallingly weak, all the strength gone from her legs, and she couldn't seem to catch her breath.

From the moment she had heard his name, she'd been functioning on automatic, her emotions fiercely contained deep inside her where they wouldn't show, determined that she wouldn't give him the satisfaction of knowing he could still shake her even after so many years. The effort had taken a terrible toll.

Alone in the harshly lighted, thick-walled, and windowless room that was cluttered with the boxes and crates holding priceless wealth, Danica tried to steady her uneven breathing and rubbed her cold hands together slowly, watching them shake. She didn't think she'd be able to withstand another confrontation with him, not without shattering into a million pieces.

Everything about the sudden meeting had been unexpected, shocking. She'd forgotten he was so tall, so . . . impressive. That his shoulders were so broad, his sable hair so thick and shining, his lean face so handsome. She'd forgotten how pale and striking his eyes were, no more than a shade darker than the finest aquamarine. She'd forgotten his intensity.

Danica allowed herself to believe the lie for only a moment. Forgotten? None of it had been forgotten.

How could she do this? Was it even possible for her to pretend she could look at him and feel nothing? She had managed to this time, but only because the shock of his appearance had frozen her.

You would have been proud of me, Dad.

The thought was a bitter one without pleasure. Her father had believed that to show emotion was to display weakness, and he had taught her well how to master hers. But Jared had devastated that control once, and Danica had little hope that ten years had armored her against him.

What would happen next time?

She had more than her own ragged emotions to cope with; he had been clearly disturbed by seeing her here, and in the few moments before he'd walked away, the fury in him had been so palpable she'd felt it. What she didn't know was whether that fierceness had been the result of anger or sheer emotional intensity a great deal more complex.

Those eyes of his glittering like tropical sunlight striking off seawater, something in them wild and savage. He had looked at her like that once before. Only once. And she had felt then just as she'd felt today, as if some terrible force, barely contained, heaved against its restraints.

How could such emotion not affect a woman?

Any woman.

Danica closed her eyes briefly as she tried to concentrate on steadying her still-ragged breathing. Her heart was beating so heavily she could feel it. She wanted to stand up but dared not make the attempt just yet. What was she sitting on? A sturdy crate, thank goodness, but what was in it? The Talisman emerald, perhaps, which legend claimed had once been worn by Merlin?

She knew the collection, every item, though only from photographs taken thirty years ago. So she remembered the Talisman emerald, an oval of one hundred and fifty carats, engraved with cryptic symbols and set into a wide bangle bracelet of solid gold. Magic, some said. Created by a wizard . . .

Concentrating on one of the pieces of this fabulous collection should have helped. Work had always steadied her, allowed her to focus on one thing to the exclusion of all else, and this opportunity to examine some of the world's most priceless treasures was certainly so rare that any gemologist would have found it mesmerizing.

My God, Dani, just look at them! her father would have said. *Hold them in your hands. Think of the history. Look at what man and nature can do together.*

She closed a door in her mind, shutting out that authoritative voice, but his presence remained smotheringly near. He would have frowned at her, she thought, when he realized that her emotional turmoil had nothing to do with the gems that surrounded her, and everything to do with the man who had just walked away.

He'd always hated Jared, though he had hidden his enmity from her.

Danica shivered slightly despite her jacket and the comfortable room. She ordered herself to stop thinking about both men, to put them out of her mind. She had a job to do, that was what she should be concentrating on. The sooner she completed that job, the sooner she could leave.

And go back to the life she had carved for herself, a life that was quiet and peaceful for the most part. Where nobody pulled at her.

"Hey, we have chairs out here, you know."

Danica was rising even as she looked toward the door, and habit made her expression calm. She liked Morgan West; an amber-eyed brunette, the young director of the *Mysteries Past* exhibit was both friendly and efficient.

"Yes, I noticed," Danica responded, her faintly ironic tone saying that the splendid luxury of the apartment had hardly escaped her observation.

Morgan grinned at her. "Max does tend to go overboard, but that's part of his charm. He and Jared just left, along with the last of the moving men."

Danica kept her features relaxed. So, he was gone again. Would he come back? Could she bear it if he did? Or if he didn't? Calmly she said, "Then the next step, I believe, is for you and me to go over the inventory together."

"That's the plan. Look, since you haven't even had a chance to unpack, I think you should go and do that while I get these boxes and crates open. By then it'll be lunchtime, and we can have something sent up while we make sure every item of the collection is present and accounted for."

That suited Danica. It would give her a bit more time to collect herself, for one thing, and to get her bearings in a strange place.

"I won't argue with that," she told Morgan, finding a path out of the crowded room as the other woman picked her way in.

"By the way," Morgan said in an innocent tone, "I

noticed Jared spent a few minutes in here a while ago. Did he happen to mention what an Interpol agent is doing hovering around the collection?"

Danica paused in the doorway and looked at the other woman. Always conscious of security, she knew better than to engage in wild speculation or even unguarded talk—but Morgan *was* the director of the exhibit and quite obviously had the complete trust of Max Bannister. Or did she?

Slowly Danica said, "I suppose he's here because the collection is quite a target for thieves."

Morgan nodded slightly. "That's what Max said when he introduced Jared to me a few days ago. And, already, we've had a bit of trouble. Early last week, there was a pretty vicious attempt made against the computer technician who's installing our security system at the museum. And there have been other problems. I'll tell you the details later. Anyway, it certainly looks like we can use all the help we can get to protect the collection."

"Then why did you ask about Jared?"

Morgan hesitated, then said lightly, "Anybody who knows me will tell you I'm curious as a cat—never happy until I find all the corners. Let's just say there are an awful lot of possibilities whenever something priceless is dangled right out in front of everybody."

Danica had always been very sensitive to undercurrents, and right now her senses were telling her that Morgan knew more about what was going on than she was prepared to tell. *Was* there a more mysterious reason for Jared's presence here? He hadn't wanted to answer her question about it, Danica remembered.

Despite her unemotional words to Jared, she wasn't interested in raising her fee if danger threatened; she accepted that possibility with every job. Where there were valuable gems the risk of trouble always existed, and Danica had grown accustomed to elaborate security arrangements long ago. Out of habit, she was always very, very careful.

But this situation was different. He was here, for one thing, his effect on her as potentially disastrous as it had been once before, and that left her tense and afraid. How could she be cautious of any outside threat when all her attention was caught up in guarding the painful vulnerability of her heart?

The silence between the two women lasted only a moment or two, and then Danica said, "Maybe we can discuss some of those possibilities. I'll go unpack, and then we can talk."

"You bet," Morgan said.

As she found her way through the spacious apartment to her bedroom, Danica couldn't help but wonder if she shouldn't just pick up her luggage and leave. It would be simpler, she thought. Safer. Probably smarter. Certainly less trouble in every sense. And no one who knew the truth would blame her a bit for leaving. In fact, of all possible options, it was the one any sane woman would choose.

And the realization had nothing to do with thieves who might be after priceless gems.

The memory of glittering aqua eyes rose in her mind, the seawater depths teeming with intensity, the power of them so incredibly potent that Danica found herself sitting on the edge of the bed, her legs gone weak again. Her heart seemed to ache every time it beat, and she couldn't catch her breath.

He wasn't even in the room and she couldn't control her response to him.

The way he'd looked at her . . . That compelling force in him focused so totally on her, she had felt it like a touch. Like a blow. Had he wanted to hit her? Or had he wanted to kiss her?

What if he came back?

What if he didn't?

They were alone in the elevator going down, and after glancing at the stone face of his companion, Max said quietly, "I couldn't help but notice a certain . . . tension . . . between you and Danica. She knows you're with Interpol?"

"Yes." Jared shoved his hands into the pockets of his jacket and stared at the doors, settling his shoulders in a restless movement as if he'd been still too long.

"Did she ask why you're here?"

Jared nodded briefly. "I told her we expected the collection to be a target. Nothing more."

After a beat, Max said, "This whole situation is difficult enough without added trouble. If there are any problems between you and Danica, I can get someone else to do the work."

Jared didn't turn his head to meet gray eyes that he knew were too perceptive. And the effort it required to hold his voice even was almost more than he could manage. But he did manage. Barely.

"No, there aren't any problems. We solved the problems a long time ago. With a divorce."

Atop another hill some blocks away, he sat in his parked car and studied the apartment building through a pair of compact binoculars. He couldn't see them, but he knew there were security people all around. There had to be. Because, of course, the collection was there. He didn't know what floor; he hadn't dared get close enough even to try to find out.

But she was there, so the collection was there, and that meant the best security money could buy.

He watched intently as the movers left—if they were movers, of course, which he doubted. Then he saw the two men come out and stand on the sidewalk for a few moments talking. The bigger man he knew from newspaper and magazine articles to be Max Bannister. He was a tough looking son-of-a-bitch— not that the other one looked like anybody you'd want to meet up with if you'd taken something he valued away from him.

He watched them, frowning. He'd expected them to guard her and the collection, of course, but this was going to be more difficult than he'd anticipated.

Or maybe not. She didn't like being shut up, he knew that; even a luxury apartment would begin to feel like a prison to her before long. So she'd leave, go out shopping or to a movie or the theater—something.

And once he had his hands on her, the security in the building wouldn't make much difference.

TWO

It was after seven that evening, and she was alone in the apartment when the soft chimes of the doorbell surprised Danica. Since she was completely aware of the security arrangements for the building, she knew that only one of the security guards or an extremely limited number of people with an encoded pass for the elevator could come up here, but she was still cautious enough to look through the spyhole in the solid oak door before making a move to open it.

Even then, she hesitated long enough for him to hit the bell again, and it was only twenty years of discipline that enabled her to square her shoulders, make her expression impassive, and open the door with a steady hand.

"May I come in?" Jared asked.

She could hear the strain in his voice, see it in the tautness of his face, and all her instincts warned

Danica that neither of them was ready for this, that it would be a mistake to admit him. But she wasn't surprised to find herself stepping back in silent acquiescence. She closed the door behind him and then led the way, still silent, into the living room.

Like all the rooms in the apartment, it was large and spacious, decorated with exquisite taste. The furniture was comfortable as well as stylish. The color scheme—mostly pale hues with splashes of very rich deeper ones in pillows and rugs—made the room seem even larger. In a modern fireplace faced with pale marble, a gas log crackled softly, and light from the reddening glow of the setting sun made the room seem warm and welcoming.

The spectacular view provided by the apartment wasn't wasted; one entire wall was floor-to-ceiling windows that provided a sweeping picture of the bay, and virtually every other room boasted equally impressive vistas.

Danica had set up her worktable in the living room, near the fireplace, and the strong light from her work lamp cast a clean, bright circle onto the surface of the table. In the white glow, lying in a nest of protective cotton, a small gold figurine studded with gems waited for her to return.

"You've started working," he noted.

"Yes, I didn't see any reason to wait." She watched as he drew a folded sheaf of papers from inside his suit jacket, and added, "What's that?"

"The inventory. After you and Morgan verified each item, Max countersigned it. And Wolfe, who's the insurance company's representative. I brought a copy back here to keep with the collection."

Danica looked at him steadily. "There was no reason for you to do that. Morgan's stopping by tomorrow morning; she could have brought it."

Jared hesitated, then dropped the papers onto the glass-topped coffee table. "Yes," he said. "She could have."

After a moment of silence, Danica moved away from him toward the kitchen. "The coffee's hot. Or would you rather have something stronger? Morgan's very efficient; this place is stocked with everything."

"Coffee's fine." Jared followed her, both relieved and a bit wry when he realized she wasn't going to taunt him about his transparent excuse to see her again. Not that derision was her style; unless she had changed a great deal in ten years, she didn't have a mocking bone in her body.

"Still take it black?" She was pouring coffee into two thick mugs, after ignoring the delicate cups he had glimpsed in the cabinet.

"Yeah." He leaned back against the counter near her, watching her. He hadn't taken his eyes off her since she had opened the door to him. She had changed out of the businesslike white suit and into casual clothing: snug jeans and a pale gold sweater, oversized, with a deep V neckline. Wearing the informal clothing, and flats instead of heels, she seemed to him more fragile, less aloof—yet still as enigmatic as a cat.

Did she feel anything? He had to wonder. Her reputation described her as utterly proficient, brisk, expert—and unemotional. Had she become as coldly brilliant as the gems she knew so well? They were born from the unimaginable pressures of the earth; had she been shaped as well by irresistible external pressures?

Had all feeling been squeezed out of her?

Instead of handing it to him, Danica pushed his coffee across the tiled counter toward him, then added cream and sugar to her mug. All her attention seemed devoted to the task, and if she felt his eyes on her, it didn't seem to disturb her. When her coffee was ready, she lifted the mug and went back to the living room.

Jared followed her once again, carrying his coffee. The silence between them wasn't doing much to ease his tension, but he was finding it virtually impossible to talk to her about casual or unimportant things. What was she thinking? Feeling? Did it disturb her at all that they had encountered each other again after so many years?

He wondered if she had taken care to avoid him before now even though their work might have been expected to draw them to the same place at least once in a decade—and probably much more often. Had she taken care that wouldn't happen? Had she consciously and deliberately avoided any chance of working with him, just as he had been careful to avoid her?

Or did she feel nothing toward him except indifference?

He had to know the answer; it was driving him crazy. Ever since he had left the building this morning, he had known he'd have to come back here to confront her, and though the hours since had provided him the time he needed to regain some of his normal control, he knew only too well that it was a tenuous control where she was concerned.

He watched her as she stood looking out, and a last ray of light from the setting sun touched her dark hair with fire. It was peculiarly indicative of her entire personality, he thought; from dark stillness and calm came a hint of passion. But only a hint. She was too controlled to give anything away.

"How have you been, Dani?" It wasn't what he wanted to ask, but at least it was a beginning.

"Fine." She half turned to look at him, her expression as unrevealing as the response. Then she shrugged. "I'm living in New York now—or, at least, I'm based there. I seem to spend most of my time on a plane."

"So you don't hate traveling after all." He heard the touch of bitterness in his comment, but he couldn't seem to control it. For an instant, he could have sworn he saw a flash of pain in the dark sheen of her eyes, but it was gone so quickly he decided he had probably imagined it.

"I think we both know that was only an excuse." She paused a beat, then said, "Is that why you came back here, Jared? To rake up the past all over again?"

"Maybe I'm just curious." He knew his rough voice belied that prosaic possibility, but went on anyway because he had to, no matter what he gave away. "It's been ten years, Daniel's gone, and you're all grown up now, Dani. So tell me. How did it all turn out? Did he win? Did Daddy's little girl grow up just the way he wanted her to?"

She moved away from the window, toward the fireplace rather than him, as if what she needed was more warmth than her coffee or the dying sun could provide. She eased down on the raised marble hearth and set her mug aside, her gaze on the bright flames.

"Winning. That's the way you always saw it, both of you. As if it was a game, some kind of competition."

The odd weariness in her response touched something inside him, but Jared had been too angry for too long to be able to push it aside now. Harshly he said, "It was supposed to be a marriage. Our marriage. But you were so busy being a daughter you never had the time to be a wife."

"Don't do this."

He ignored the almost inaudible plea. Setting his unwanted coffee down on an end table, he took a few hasty steps until he was standing only a couple of feet away from her, looming over her because she was sitting. She looked so damned fragile and defenseless, and that made him even angrier. It made him feel like a total bastard for just raising his voice to her, but he couldn't stop because the frustration and bitterness inside him demanded an outlet.

It had been like that before, he remembered. Her great, wounded eyes staring up at him in bewilderment, her voice unsteady, as she begged him to try to understand the duty she felt to her father. Flinching a bit, but not backing away from his furious resentment, not fidgeting even in her agitation because Daniel couldn't bear anyone to fidget around him and he'd rid her of nervous mannerisms long before her teens.

External pressures, Jared thought bleakly, shaping her like the cold, hard earth shaped a diamond from carbon.

Daniel. The old bastard had been larger than life, his hold on his young daughter as soft as velvet and as unyielding as solid iron. A master manipulator, he had used every opportunity to make Jared seem harsh and unreasonable, until finally Danica had begun to pull away from her demanding husband. . . .

"I want to know, Dani," Jared said roughly. "I want to know if you ever learned to see past his charade. Or did he have you fooled right up to the end?"

"*Stop it.*" She was on her feet suddenly, those dark eyes glittering as she stared up at him, her lovely face transformed into something even more beautiful and passionate by the animation of powerful emotions.

Her hands were fists at her sides, her slender body rigid with sheer anger.

Jared knew then, in that instant, that Daniel had lost. *Lost.* Danica had become her own woman. He wasn't even sure he was breathing as he stared at her, and at first her shaking words barely penetrated his mind.

"I'm not seventeen anymore, Jared. And I won't tear myself apart again trying to please two men fighting over me like dogs with a bone—especially when one of them is dead."

Slowly Jared said, "I was your husband."

"And he was my father! For seventeen years the only man in my life, the only parent, my teacher . . . my friend. Whatever you think of him, he was the center of my life." She drew a quick breath. "But then you came along, didn't you? As young as he was old, as intense as he was composed—and you were so damned sure of yourself. You turned my world upside down, and before I knew what was happening, we were married. A marriage my father approved, remember?"

"He only approved because he knew you'd run off with me if he didn't," Jared snapped, the old anger returning even though this new spirit of hers was so riveting he could hardly think of anything else.

Danica wasn't so angry that she didn't recognize the truth when she heard it, but the cork was out of the bottle now and she couldn't contain the fury spilling out. "What difference does that make? The two of you were so determined to compete with each other, it didn't matter when you began."

"Dammit, it was *his* scheming, can't you see that even now? He approved our marriage so he wouldn't alienate you, but he made sure he kept control of the situation. Those so-reasonable conditions of his designed purely to keep you bound to him. He wanted to continue passing on his life's skills to you, so of course he had to live near us in Paris. And the work he'd chosen for you—"

"I chose it for myself," Danica interrupted fiercely.

Jared went on as if she hadn't. "—required intense study, so of course you had to spend every day in his workshop. And you couldn't leave town, couldn't go on a trip with your husband, because Daniel would turn into a sickly old man right in front of your eyes and make you feel guilty for abandoning him."

"He was past sixty," she reminded him in a shaking voice.

"And so frail you couldn't leave him for more than a night? Come off it, Dani, you have to know better than that. He wasn't sick a day of his life. He'd still be alive today, strong as a bull, if he hadn't lost control of his car on a slippery road three years ago. He was manipulating you, was out to destroy our marriage from the very day he gave his approval."

"Does that excuse you?" she demanded. "Did it make you better than him because he started the fight, even though you helped him turn our marriage into a battleground?"

"All I wanted was my wife," Jared said shortly.

"Maybe it started out that way, but before long what you really wanted, what you tried to do constantly, was to defeat Daniel Gray. To beat him. To win. Just like he was trying to defeat you. An old man and a young man fighting each other, using me like a weapon, because the battle meant more to you both than I did."

Jared's angry denial died in his throat as he stared at her pale face, into the turbulent dark eyes. Was she right? Could it really have been as much his fault as Daniel's? Had his own youth and inexperience led him to make the colossal blunder of trying to compete with the one man on earth he should never have treated as a rival—the father of the woman he loved?

"It was him," Jared said, unable to accept the burden of blame so easily. "He was the one who made constant demands, insisting you spend so much time with him and then sending work home with you to make sure you had no time for me. He was the one who never had a good thing to say about me, poisoning you against me, making you draw away from me. He was the only one trying to compete, trying to hold on to you—"

"It was both of you." Danica's voice was still unsteady, but quieter now, and her lovely face was strained with emotion. "He wanted a daughter, you wanted a wife—and neither of you could bear to have less than all of me, all my attention, all my time. All my love." She drew a quick breath, her eyes glittering now with tears. "And I was a seventeen-year-old girl who didn't know how to handle either one of you."

He watched her sit back down on the hearth suddenly as if her legs had given out on her, and he began to realize that what had happened more than ten years ago had been far more complicated than he'd always believed. After listening to her—something he wouldn't have been able to do then even if she had been able to explain her feelings—it didn't seem so easy now to assign blame in the destruction of their marriage, to find a target for his bitterness.

Was Danica to blame? Daniel had been her only family since birth, when her mother had died in a Boston hospital after giving their daughter life, and he had taken her with him wherever his abilities as a world-renowned gemologist had sent him. Raised by one older—forty-five when she was born—and strong-willed parent, molded by him into a dutiful daughter and a willing pupil to absorb the knowledge he wanted to pass on to his child, could she have done anything but what she *had*—tried to please both men but giving in most often to the father who'd guided her for seventeen years?

Had Daniel been to blame? Yes, he'd been a master manipulator, old enough to be subtle and patient, and with a more certain knowledge of his daughter than the younger man could claim, but had he really done anything more terrible than Jared had done himself—tried to hold on to what he loved because he was terrified of losing her to another man?

Or was he to blame? Obsessed with Danica, competitive and a bit selfish at twenty-four years of age, Jared had never given much thought to how young she had been, how sheltered—or how strongly bound she was to a dominating father. He had known only that he loved fiercely, wanted desperately, and it was in the nature of all young male creatures to grab what they desired and hold on furiously when a threat was sensed.

As if she read his mind, Danica said, "Does it really matter whose fault it was?" She was looking into the fire once more, her face still again but tense, no longer the detached mask. Her breathing was a bit uneven, as if the turmoil of her own emotions had torn at her physically. "The entire crux of the problem, I think, is that I was too young. Too young for you, and too young to let go of my father. I didn't understand what was happening, not then. All I knew was that you were both pulling at me. And it hurt."

Those last three words, almost whispered and unsteady with pain, destroyed the last of Jared's reluctance to let go of his corrosive anger. He suddenly felt exhausted and a bit numb. It was disturbing to realize that a terrible pain he could still feel and ten years of bitterness might have sprung from a simple case of bad timing.

Sitting down on the hearth a foot or so away from her, the heat of the fire at his back, Jared said slowly, "I should have waited, given you more time. Gone back to Paris and left you in London with Daniel, at least for another year or two. I knew you were too young to be married, but . . . hell, I didn't care. I wanted you too much to be able to see anything else. Even your fear of me."

Danica met his gaze, recognizing the diffident but vital question in his unforgettable eyes. "It wasn't fear," she said slowly. "You did make me nervous, though. You were so intense, so confident. About everything, but especially about me. Sometimes I felt overwhelmed. It was exciting, and scary, too. But even when you yelled at me, I was never afraid you'd hit me or anything."

"There are other ways to hurt," Jared murmured.

She couldn't deny that, and nodded. "The worst of it, to me, was that you and Dad didn't seem to realize how hard I was trying to please both of you; that didn't count for anything, apparently. You were always so angry, and he was different since I met you, more demanding. I couldn't seem to do anything right and I was tense all the time."

"I know. I could see it, but by then I'd realized you were beginning to draw away from me—which I blamed Daniel for—and I was so busy trying to hold on to you that everything just got worse."

She hesitated, then looked away from him and said softly, "I didn't know what to do. You and I didn't talk anymore, and what little time we had together had turned into nothing but tension and anger. I even began dreading going home at night, dreading being with you and . . . and dreading our lovemaking, because I could feel that you wanted something from me, something that was missing . . . and I didn't know what it was. I thought there was something wrong with me."

For a moment Jared could only stare at her averted face, feeling stunned. He reached over slowly, brushing back the curtain of silky dark hair half veiling her face from his gaze. His fingers lingered, resting on the side of her neck, where her skin was soft and warm and a pulse throbbed quickly.

"There was nothing wrong with you. It was just . . . You were right, I wanted all of you. All your love. Your time and attention. Everything I thought you were holding back from me. And—"

She looked at him, hesitant but direct. "And?"

He didn't want to answer yet, even more, he didn't want this painful honesty between them to end. It was difficult to hold his voice steady, especially with his hand touching her and another kind of memory filling his mind, but he tried.

"And I think there *was* something missing—but it was my fault, not yours. I wanted you to feel what I did when we made love, and I never stopped to remember how young you were. If I'd been more patient . . . if I hadn't overwhelmed you with my own feelings . . . if I'd allowed you the time you needed . . . then maybe your response to me would have been different."

"Different, how?"

Gazing into her liquid dark eyes, his heart pounding in a sudden intense burst of relief and something else, something he didn't stop to contemplate, Jared wondered if she realized what she had just told him. Then he answered that himself, silently. No, she didn't. If she had realized, she wouldn't have needed to ask the question.

Huskily he said, "Dani, I know you felt pleasure when we made love, but it was . . . mild compared to what I felt. And compared to what you *could* have felt. If you'd been older, or if I had been more patient. At first you were shy and a little frightened, and after that there was so much tension between us you couldn't relax with me, couldn't let yourself go."

She remembered that well, and Danica felt a new heat in her face that had nothing to do with the closeness of the fire. The nights with Jared were vivid in her mind, even now. The hunger of his lovemaking, her dazed response. And even though she *had* been too overwhelmed by him and his emotions, and too immature both physically and emotionally to have been able to feel more than the first hesitant stirrings of the sensations a woman's body was capable of, that alone had been powerful enough to have lingered all these years.

He had been a part of her life so briefly, only one cycle of the seasons, and yet he had changed her forever.

Danica gazed into his hypnotic eyes and wondered vaguely what he'd say if she told him that she still woke in the night sometimes and found herself listening for the sound of his breathing, reaching out for the warmth of his body. But she didn't tell him that, of course.

"Like I said, you made me nervous," she murmured.

"I'm sorry about that," he said, his vivid eyes very intent on her face. "Especially since I really think we could have survived any outside pressure if the bond between us had been strong enough."

Danica shook her head a little, the movement making her even more conscious of his hand at her neck, the touch of him warm and hard. "That might have been true, but it would have had to be more than a physical bond." She kept her voice quiet and steady with an effort.

"We had more than that."

"No." She hesitated, though all her instincts told her they could move forward from this point only if both of them understood all the reasons they had failed the first time. She didn't know if Jared wanted that, or even if she did. The very prospect frightened her a little, because she knew it would disturb her hard-won control no matter how it ended, wrecking the peace of her life. But she felt compelled to keep going, driven by something she couldn't even define.

"Dani—"

She shook her head again. "No, we didn't have more than that. Be honest, Jared."

He was frowning slightly. "We had a great deal in common. My work was in locating and recovering stolen artworks and gems, while you were well on your way to being an expert gemologist and specialist in fakes and forgeries."

"Yes," Danica said. "We had that in common, our work. But what did you really know about me? My favorite color? The music I preferred? The kinds of movies I liked? What was my favorite flower?"

"Roses," he muttered, remembering.

Her smile was a bit twisted. "No. Dad's favorite, but not mine. It's ironic, but you probably knew more about him than you did about me."

Jared wanted to deny it, but once again he was conscious of the leaden feeling that came with accepting an uncomfortable truth. "Did you know much about me?"

"No," Danica replied quietly. "Virtually nothing of likes and dislikes. And all I knew of your family was that your mother was American, your father French, that you had a dual citizenship. We married so quick-ly there wasn't time for anyone to be invited to the ceremony. . . ."

Jared answered the implied question. "Dad's an archaeologist and a collector—paintings mostly. As I recall, he was somewhere in the Orient that year. Right now he's in Peru."

"And your mother?"

"She travels too. Only in her case, it's simply a restless need to see and do everything imaginable. She never has an itinerary, and I learned to stop worrying about her before I was out of my teens." He hesi-tated, then went on evenly, "When my letter about our marriage caught up with her, she called from somewhere—Alaska, I think—and said she was drop-ping everything and flying to Paris to meet her new daughter-in-law. I told her not to bother. The ink was just about dry on the divorce papers."

Danica was silent for a moment. There was noth-ing she could say about that, no words to change the pain and bitterness he must have felt. Instead she said, "We never talked like this then. Why not, Jared? Didn't we want to know about each other?"

He wanted to say, but couldn't, that he had known the essence of her. Her gentleness and calm. Her sweetness. The graceful, deliberate way she moved. The silkiness of her skin and the softness of her touch and the music of her voice. That was what he had known.

"We were strangers," she continued. "Your mother must have been shocked. . . . Do you realize that from the first day you walked into Dad's workshop until the day you filed for divorce was less than a year?"

"Yes, I've thought about it. So quickly. Sometimes . . . it feels as if it all happened in a matter of weeks. But then I can remember the passing seasons."

Danica remembered as well, and struggled not to let the memories overwhelm her. "Strangers," she repeated. "It's probably a miracle we lasted even that long."

Jared looked at her, his vibrant eyes narrowing a bit. For an instant, she thought the memories *were* overwhelming her, but then she realized this was no memory. He was gazing at her in that intense, mesmerizing way, all his attention focused completely on her, and her heart began to slam against her ribs in a response she couldn't control.

"Strangers?" His low voice was reflective, considering. "I don't think so, Dani. Whatever we were, it was much more than that."

Before she could even begin to frame a response, he slid his hand around to the nape of her neck, underneath her hair, and drew her toward him as he moved to close the narrow distance between them. His head bent, and his mouth covered hers.

She stiffened almost instinctively, but she knew she didn't have a hope of resisting him. However timid or tense she might have been with him during their marriage, the unquestionable truth was that her body had never known another man, and his touch had never been forgotten.

His mouth was warm and hard, moving over hers with a slow, potent seduction that made her stiffness melt, her body soften and sway toward his. She realized that she had reached out to him only when she felt the slight roughness of his jacket under her fingers and the smooth material of his white shirt under her thumbs. The hardness of his body, even through his clothing, was unexpectedly familiar.

Danica thought she heard a little sound and dimly recognized it as coming from her throat. Every nerve in her body was alive, throbbing, and there was a new heat inside her, surging beyond her ability to control. She responded helplessly, her mouth opening beneath the increasing force of his, and when his tongue glided between her lips, the sensual possession of the caress was both shocking and wildly exciting.

She didn't remember this, didn't remember the power of the longing filling her, this growing hunger for him that was so profound it was terrifying. Even as she struggled to cope with the astonishing sensations and overwhelming emotions, Danica realized that this was what Jared had meant when he had said her response to him all those years ago might have been different if she had been older or if he had been more patient with her.

He lifted his head at last, and even though she was dazed, she could see he felt the power of what was between them as intensely as she did. His lean face was taut, his eyes darkened like the sea before a storm, and his breathing was as uneven as hers.

"Strangers?" he repeated huskily. "No, Dani. I couldn't feel like this about a stranger."

She wanted to ask him what he felt, but the words wouldn't emerge past her tight throat. And with her own feelings in turmoil, every instinct warned her not to move too hastily. She needed time, time to get her bearings. Whatever happened between her and Jared, she refused to be swept along without a moment to think.

With a reluctance she knew he could see, she took her hands off him and then slowly pulled away from him. She got to her feet and went to the closest window, gazing out without really seeing much. It was getting dark, the lights of the city winking far below.

Danica wondered if she was strong enough for this. Losing him once had nearly killed her. What if it happened again? What if they discovered, in the end, that they were one of those couples who wanted each other wildly and yet simply couldn't manage to be together?

"Dani?"

He was there, right behind her, and she wanted to throw herself into his arms, leave the questions unanswered until they had to be. Instead she turned slowly and looked up at him, wondering if it was all in her eyes, the doubts and longings, the excitement and the terror. Probably, she thought.

"What is it you want, Jared?" she asked unsteadily. "Do you want me to admit there's still something between us? I can't deny that. But when we were together before, it was tense, and painful, and I can't go through that again."

"It'll be different this time, Dani." His voice was low, but the confidence she remembered so well from before was in him, in the glint of his eyes and the curve of his smile. He was so sure of himself. . . .

"Why? Because Dad's gone?"

"Because we're older and wiser. Because we value each other and what we feel. And because I mean to fight like hell to make *sure* it's different this time."

His determination, that assured strength, was partly why she had fallen in love with him so long ago, but Danica *was* older now, with a much more secure sense of herself—and she wasn't about to be swept off her feet.

Quietly she said, "The only thing I'm sure of is that I won't let you turn my life upside down again. I'm not a girl anymore, Jared, and the only person I have to please now is myself. What makes you think I'd want to change that?"

"Because you felt what I did a few minutes ago," he told her flatly.

Danica didn't let that truth sway her. "I still remember what I felt years ago, looking at divorce papers. And before that, what I felt every time you were angry with me." She drew a quick breath. "It isn't so simple as you seem to think to just . . . pick up where we left off."

Jared lifted a hand as if to touch her, but let it fall back to his side. "I know that, and I wouldn't want to. Dani, we have to start over again, at the beginning."

She shook her head a little, unsure of his meaning. "How can we? With all that happened—"

"Listen to me." His voice was very steady, and his eyes never wavered from her face. "I know that neither of us can forget what happened before, but there *is* still something between us, something too rare to throw away. It's worth a second chance."

His intensity touched her, just as it always had, and she wanted to ask him why it was so important to him that they try again. But she was still unwilling to ask him how he really felt, hesitant to question her own feelings, and most of all, reluctant to give way and allow him to dominate her the way he had before with his strength and conviction.

She wouldn't be swept off her feet again.

Danica drew a short breath, her tenuous control slipping a bit. Those eyes of his, so damn hypnotic, compelling her to give in to him . . . God, had it been this difficult all those years ago to say no to him?

"Jared, I need—I *want*—time to think. If there was one hard lesson I learned from that year in my life, it was that I have to make up my own mind about anything that affects me."

Again, it seemed that he would touch her, but he never completed the gesture. There was something impatient in his expressive eyes, but also enough anxiety to temper the rougher emotion. "You aren't saying no?"

Danica kept her voice quiet and even. "I'm saying that it's been a long day, and I'd like to be alone now."

For a moment, she thought he would demand a more direct answer to his question, but finally he nodded. Whether he realized she was on the fine edge of her control or simply chose to give in to her plea for more time, it was obvious he was stepping back only because she asked, not because he wanted to.

He got as far as the doorway of the living room before he turned to look at her. It was an oddly fierce look, but his voice was very soft.

"What is your favorite flower, Dani?"

She managed a shaky smile. "I love orchids."

Jared nodded slightly, then left the apartment without another word. This time she knew he was coming back. But she still didn't know if she could bear it.

THREE

After a restless night, Danica was up early, forcing herself to begin adjusting to a new time zone. A hot shower and breakfast helped drive away the cobwebs in her mind, and by the time she'd neatened the kitchen and carried her coffee into the living room, she was ready to go to work. At least, she thought she was.

She turned on the television to an early news program—more because she disliked total silence than anything else—and settled down at her worktable. It was her habit to focus all her concentration on what she was doing, closing out any outside distractions. However, for the first time in years, the distraction Danica felt wasn't outside herself but was due to her own emotions.

Jared. He had come back into her life at a point when she'd finally achieved a serene balance, where her work and her private life were peaceful and under her control. As she'd told him, the only one she had to please now was herself. But Danica didn't feel very peaceful or serene now, and the truth was that she didn't know what would please her.

Was she willing to make herself vulnerable to him again? To risk the potential pain of any kind of involvement with her ex-husband? They had become two different people, both older, and she thought they had a better understanding of why their marriage had failed. Though he'd been obviously bitter and had wanted to blame both her and her father for what had happened, Danica thought Jared no longer felt that way.

Which was not to say that his anger at her and his strong dislike—perhaps even hatred—of her father had vanished. It would take time for that to happen, if it ever did. And it was quite possible that Jared's emotions in the meantime could prove painful to her.

As if that wasn't enough to make her hesitate, her feelings toward Jared were definitely confused. Memories of the strain and unhappiness of ten years ago tangled with memories of how much she had loved him even through all the pain and bewilderment of those final months together. And now, knowing that desire still existed between them—stronger than it had ever been during their marriage in Danica's case—she was both tempted to explore new possibilities and terrified of being hurt again.

A part of her wanted to cling to the safety and peace of her life without Jared, to fight his insistence or just leave, run away. But a voice from deep inside her warned that she couldn't hide from him any more than she could hide from life, and since the longing he had ignited with a touch had haunted her dreams last night, she doubted she would be able to withstand Jared's insistence if he remained so determined.

Lost in thought and anxiety, she didn't realize how long she'd sat there at her worktable, hands folded, until she looked idly at the television and found that a game show had replaced the morning news program. She glanced at her watch, and winced when she realized she had been sitting there for more than an hour without getting a damned thing accomplished.

Before she could do more than silently berate herself, the doorbell rang, and Danica felt her heartbeat quicken until she remembered that Morgan was due about this time. Sure enough, it was Morgan, and as usual she was talkative and slightly harassed.

She was also bearing flowers.

"They aren't from me," she said cheerfully as she handed over a slim crystal vase filled with delicate orchids. "The delivery guy came in downstairs just as I was about to come up, so I volunteered. Hit me if I'm being too nosy, but since very few people are supposed to know you're in San Francisco, and since Max is happily married and Wolfe happily engaged, I figure these have to be from Jared."

"Good guess," Danica murmured, setting the vase on the coffee table and removing a small white envelope from among the airy blooms. She sat down on the couch while Morgan settled in the comfortable chair nearby. Opening the envelope, Danica recognized Jared's handwriting on the card, which was another shock—God, hadn't ten years dimmed any of her memories?—and her eyes seemed to blur just a bit before she was able to focus on the words.

May I take you to lunch? One o'clock. Jared.

Danica felt her lips twist slightly even as her heartbeat quickened. Damn him. It might have been a request, but he clearly expected her to accept. Briefly she wished she could summon the will to refuse, but wasn't very surprised to hear herself ask Morgan a mild question.

"You and Max have made sure I'd have everything I needed here in the apartment. Does security demand that I stay here all the time?"

"No, of course not," Morgan answered promptly, confirming Danica's expectation. "We'd all prefer that you keep a low profile since you're so well-known as an expert gemologist, but you're certainly free to come and go as you please."

Since Jared had always been an excellent police officer, Danica had been certain that not even strong personal feelings would have compelled him to do something against any of his professional demands; if it had been in the best interests of the Bannister collection for her to remain closeted here twenty-four hours a day, he never would have suggested that she go out. Even with him.

"As a matter of fact," Morgan went on, "I was going to suggest you visit the museum sometime in the next day or so. I'd like your opinion on the display cases we've installed for the collection, for one thing. Besides, the museum has some great exhibits aside from *Mysteries Past*, and you should meet everyone involved with Max's collection."

Danica nodded. "I'd like to."

Shrewdly Morgan said, "But today you have a date. Right?"

"A lunch date, apparently." Danica didn't realize there was a touch of resentment in her voice until Morgan grinned at her.

"Jared's being a little high-handed?"

"A little." Danica smiled and, after a slight hesitation, added, "To do him justice, I think it's more impatience than arrogance. At least . . . that's the way he used to be."

Morgan looked satisfied rather than surprised. "My intuition told me it was glowing embers rather than a new fire with you two."

"That's a colorful way to put it."

"But accurate?" Morgan probed.

Danica didn't see any reason for her to hide or deny her past relationship with Jared, and besides, she found it amazingly comfortable to confide in the other woman. "I guess you could say that. Ten years ago I was his wife."

That did startle Morgan. "Ten years ago you couldn't have been out of high school," she protested.

Danica slipped the little card back into its envelope and dropped it onto the coffee table. "I was. Barely. We met, and married, when I was seventeen. Divorced a year later."

Morgan's golden eyes held sympathy. "That must have been rough on both of you. Especially you. At seventeen, we feel *so much*—and don't understand a damned thing."

"That is certainly true." Danica smiled. "But water under the bridge, as they say."

"Maybe not. You're here, he's here—and you've got a lunch date. It looks like neither one of you burned that bridge."

"We'll see." Danica certainly wasn't willing to believe there was a future for her and Jared. Not now, anyway. Not yet. "The coffee's hot, would you like some?"

Morgan grimaced slightly. "I'd love some, but I can't stay. There are a million things waiting for me at the museum. I didn't even intend to sit down. All I wanted to do was bring you these forms from the insurance company—I just got sidetracked by the flowers." The thick manila envelope had been tucked under her arm, almost forgotten.

Danica accepted the envelope and slid the forms out, studying them, trying to focus on business. "They seem clear enough," she murmured. Since each piece of the Bannister collection was being reappraised prior to the opening of the exhibit, these were the forms Lloyd's of London required to be completed. They weren't unfamiliar to her.

"Yeah, I thought so," Morgan said. "By the way, Max said to tell you that nobody expects you to work around the clock. The exhibit is due to open in four weeks, but that isn't written in stone."

Danica eyed her somewhat ruefully. "It's certainly written in the public mind. I saw articles about *Mysteries Past* a month ago in New York, and I personally know at least half a dozen collectors and gemologists who already have their tickets to fly out here the week of the opening."

Morgan chuckled. "Yeah, I know. You wouldn't believe the calls I've been fielding from all over the world. And the museum hung a banner outside the front door *more* than a month ago announcing the forthcoming exhibit. Be that as it may, *Mysteries Past* will open to the public when Maxim Bannister says it will, and not a minute sooner. So just don't feel pressured to work too hard."

Smiling, Danica said, "I appreciate the concern. But you can tell Max that I should have the collection ready to be transferred to the museum in about two weeks, even working no more than six or eight hours a day."

Rising to her feet, Morgan chuckled again. "Even with an impatient Interpol cop dragging you off to lunch from time to time?"

As she accompanied her visitor to the door Danica answered, "I think I can manage to find eight hours out of every twenty-four to work in spite of most outside distractions." She wondered silently if she believed that.

Morgan didn't comment, but merely said, "Well, you have my number at the museum, Max's private number—and I'm sure Jared's going to keep in touch. If anything comes up, one of us should be able to help."

Danica returned to her worktable after the other woman had left, determinedly focusing her mind on the two-hundred-carat Midnight sapphire, which had to be delicately cleaned and painstakingly appraised. She set her mental alarm for noon to allow her time to get ready to leave with Jared, then refused to let thoughts of him disturb her concentration.

At noon, still trying not to think very much, she halted her work, put the piece away in the apartment's safe room, and went to change into something a little less casual than her jeans and sweater. Bearing in mind the extremely variable weather of San Francisco, she opted for slacks instead of a skirt, worn with a silk blouse and a lightweight blazer. She was aware that the outfit was one of the more severe, tailored choices she could have made, but since she was still feeling decidedly uncertain about the entire situation, she wasn't about to play up her femininity for Jared's eyes.

What she didn't realize, simply because there was no vanity in her nature, was that she could hardly help but be totally feminine no matter what she wore. It was something Jared definitely noticed the moment she opened the door to him, but he didn't comment.

"The flowers are lovely," she said. "Thank you."

"I never knew there were so many varieties of orchids," he responded lightly. "The florist tried to sell me on some type that looked like a spider, but I passed."

"I appreciate that."

"They still bother you?" He was smiling slightly.

Her childhood fear of spiders had lingered, and he obviously remembered. "Afraid so. I don't go into a blind panic anymore, but I definitely don't like them."

"We each have our phobias," he murmured.

He hadn't stepped inside, so Danica picked up her purse from the hall table and joined him in the outer foyer. She didn't much like discussing her phobias with Jared; it made her feel unnervingly vulnerable. And it reminded her of something she would have preferred to avoid facing. Though he might not know her favorite color or music, the simple truth was that Jared knew things about her no other man on earth could know.

She thrust the realization into a room in her mind and slammed the door on it. Control, she knew, was her only defense against Jared. She had to remain calm and in control, to guide their conversations away from personal matters.

It was the only hope she had of keeping him at arm's length. She couldn't allow him to overwhelm her again, to sweep her up into an emotional turbulence that could, as it had before, leave her shattered and anguished.

And without him.

Locking the door carefully behind her, she said, "I made sure the safe room is locked up tight, with every piece of the collection inside it. No one said to, but I assume I should do so whenever I'm not actually working and when I leave the apartment."

Jared nodded as she turned back to face him. In the same businesslike tone she had used, he said, "Yes, and there's another procedure I'd like you to follow. Whenever you leave the building, always tell the guards downstairs where you're going and when you expect to return."

Danica didn't respond to that until they stood in the descending elevator. Jared was holding her arm lightly and she was trying not to be so conscious of the contact.

"What's the reasoning behind that?" she asked mildly. "As long as the collection is sealed up here, how can my whereabouts influence security?"

Jared's long fingers tightened just a little on her arm, but his voice remained impersonal. "The world of art and gems is a relatively small one, and those interested tend to know all the players. It is conceivable that you could be recognized by someone after the collection, someone smart enough to put your presence here together with the upcoming exhibit— and arrive at a reasonable conclusion. It's also conceivable that you could be seen as a tool."

Danica was watching the elevator's control panel, absently noting the light behind each floor's number as they descended toward the lobby. "I wouldn't be a very good tool," she said calmly.

"But a thief wouldn't know that until he had his hands on you, would he?" Jared responded, his seeming indifference belied by the tension growing in his voice. "He wouldn't know the security setup here until he got the information out of you. He wouldn't know that the guards are under orders to allow absolutely no one not already known to them past the lobby, with or without a security card."

"All right, point taken. I'll tell the guards where I'm going and when I expect to return." She thought silently that doing so wouldn't prevent a would-be thief from grabbing her, it would only alert the guards that something had happened when she didn't return as expected.

Jared must have been thinking along the same lines; his tension was far more obvious when he spoke abruptly. "Dani, for your own safety, you shouldn't leave this building alone. Alone, you're too tempting a target if you are recognized, too vulnerable. I'll be glad to take you anywhere you want to go, anytime you ask. Promise me you won't leave on your own."

Danica was spared the need to respond immediately since the elevator door opened onto the lobby just then. In silence, they walked across to the guards' desk. Jared released her arm to sign the security log, and while she added her signature to his he told the guards flatly that he would be responsible for her until he brought her back to the building.

He didn't, Danica noted, tell the guards where they were going or when they would return.

"Yes, sir," the older of the two guards said, his face impassive.

She remained silent as Jared took her arm again and guided her from the building. Outside, the faint chill of the breeze was offset by cheerful sunshine, and Danica looked around idly as they walked across the pavement to where his car was parked in the circular drive in front of the building.

They were being watched. She could feel it. It wasn't obvious, of course, but she didn't doubt several pairs of eyes surveyed the building constantly, around the clock, noting the comings and goings of residents and visitors. One didn't take stupid chances with something as priceless as the Bannister collection, after all.

When he opened the door of a rather ordinary, nondescript sedan for her, she got in, then waited silently while he went around the car to get in on the driver's side.

"Dani? You haven't promised."

He hadn't started the car, and she knew he wouldn't until she answered him. "Morgan told me I was free to come and go as I pleased," she said neutrally.

"Look at me."

She wanted to resist that command—it certainly hadn't been a request—but couldn't. The best she could do was keep her expression calm when she turned her head toward him. He looked as tense as he had sounded, his mouth a thin line and his pale eyes fierce.

"I don't want anything to happen to you," he said softly. "Do you understand? I've seen the lengths some thieves and collectors will go to, and it's a risk I don't want to take. Not with you. You have to see there's no sense in taking chances, Dani. Don't let your pride win out over common sense."

It *had* been her pride that had balked, along with her uneasy fear of losing her hard-won independence. But as much as she wanted to struggle against giving in to him—on anything—she couldn't help but see he was right.

Finally she nodded. "I won't leave the building alone." She hesitated, but couldn't help adding, "I imagine Morgan would be quite willing to show me something of the city. If I asked."

Jared smiled slightly, but his eyes remained intense. "Anybody but me, I gather? Is it because you don't want to be with me, Dani, or because you don't want to have to ask me for anything?"

Again, he had struck a nerve in her, unerringly pinpointing her emotions and motivations. And though a part of her wanted to lie about it, the painful honesty they had found the night before compelled her to tell him the truth.

Carefully she answered, "I'm not sure if I want to be with you yet. And I don't know if I could ask you for anything—even your company."

His smile faded a bit. "Well, that's honest."

"You want me to be honest, don't you?"

"Want?" He considered the word for a moment in silence while he continued to gaze at her, his hand on the steering wheel flexing restlessly. Then, his voice roughening, he said, "What I want is to have you look at me with unguarded eyes. To have you trust me the way you once did. So, yes, I want us to be honest with each other. No matter how much it hurts."

Danica dropped her gaze briefly to the hands folded sedately in her lap, then looked at him again. "All right. But I hope you'll try to remember something, Jared. Ten years is a long time. And I'm a long way from that girl you first saw in Dad's workshop. My life *is* my life now. I make my own decisions. And I won't be rushed into anything."

"Is that what you're afraid of? That I'll push you into a relationship you aren't ready for?"

"Partly." With an effort, her gaze and her voice remained steady. "Already it's like before. You're so sure . . . and I'm not."

"I can't help how I feel," he said.

Danica didn't ask him to explain his feelings, shying away from them even though she didn't move. "I can't help how I feel, either. Jared . . . you're the one who said we had to start over, at the beginning. Beginnings should be slow."

He sighed a bit roughly. "As I remember, our first beginning was about as slow as a tidal wave."

"And look what happened."

Jared's fingers tightened on the steering wheel, but after a moment he faced forward and started the engine. His voice was low, reluctant but determined. "All right, Dani. I'll do my best not to push, not to rush you. But don't expect me to pretend we're strangers. No matter what you say, I don't believe that's true."

Unfortunately for her peace of mind, Danica didn't believe it either.

Lunch, which took place at a cheerful waterfront restaurant, was almost relaxed and fairly casual. Jared made an effort, keeping their conversation aimed toward the careful process of getting to know each other, and Danica was more than happy to assist him in that. So they talked about what each of them had been doing during the past few years, briefly touching on various assignments and locations.

Each of them understood the other's job quite well, and that provided a kind of anchor for them. From that central core of knowledge, they explored outward cautiously.

Danica had forgotten what a pleasant companion Jared could be when he cloaked his intensity and turned on the charm. He even made her laugh more than once, and she was a little surprised to find that she thoroughly enjoyed being with him.

The man was definitely dangerous.

It wasn't until they reached the coffee-and-dessert stage of the meal that the subject returned to the Bannister collection and the forthcoming *Mysteries Past* exhibit, and it was Danica who was responsible for that.

Since the lunch crowd had thinned, there was no one near their table, but she nonetheless lowered her voice when she said, "It isn't usual for a senior Interpol agent to stand guard over anything, no matter how valuable, and Max Bannister hardly needs official help when he could raise an army of his own to protect his property. What are you really doing here, Jared?"

After a brief silence, he smiled wryly. "Something my superiors will definitely not approve of—especially if it doesn't work."

"If what doesn't work?"

"Our trap. Once installed in the museum, the collection is going to be bait, Dani. Very tempting bait, to catch a very elusive thief."

Danica frowned slightly. While she and Morgan had inventoried the collection together the day before, the other woman had told her much of what had gone on during the past few weeks—including her own midnight meeting with an infamous cat burglar named Quinn and their subsequent adventures.

"I'm going to see him in the sunshine one of these days," Morgan had muttered. "I live for that."

Now, studying her companion as she sipped her coffee, Danica wondered if Morgan suspected a trap was being set for her Quinn. She hadn't said so, but she had been just a bit too curious about Jared's involvement with the exhibit, despite her casual air about it. And though Danica didn't consider herself unusually perceptive, she was certain that the young director of the *Mysteries Past* exhibit was in the painful process of falling hard for the charming but enigmatic thief.

"You're awfully silent," Jared murmured.

"Just thinking." She set her cup down. "I can see how Interpol might be a bit upset with you. And I imagine Lloyd's of London wouldn't be very pleased if they knew about the trap. I guess I'm most surprised at Max being willing to take the risk. It took his family five centuries to build the collection, and every piece is irreplaceable."

"Don't remind me. I think it's a lunatic idea and I have from the beginning."

"Then it wasn't your idea. Why did you agree to it?"

"Max agreed. Once he did, there was nothing I could do about it except go along."

Danica started to ask him just who had come up with the idea in the first place, but Jared glanced at his watch and added, "Speaking of Max, he suggested you visit the museum this afternoon, if you aren't too tired."

"I need to be working," she protested.

"Dani, what you need is to give yourself time to adjust to a new time zone. You flew over from Europe, didn't you?"

"Yes, but—"

"Then you've got to be jet-lagged. We both know the work you do is extremely detailed and painstaking; it demands a clear and rested mind. Besides, Max fully expects you to take a day or two to get acclimated; that's why he suggested you see the museum today."

She wavered, telling herself he was right even though a little voice in her head scolded her for wasting a perfectly good afternoon. When she recognized the voice as her father's, however, she immediately chose to ignore it.

"All right, then."

"Good." Jared smiled at her and then signaled the

waitress to bring the check. "And on the way, I can show you a little of the city."

"You aren't a native," Danica murmured.

"No, but I've learned my way around during the past few weeks, so I think I'll make a decent guide."

Danica wouldn't have bet against him; if there was one thing that hadn't changed in ten years, it was Jared's confidence in himself. It was an oddly seductive thing, that confidence, and immensely distracting. So much so that she forgot all about the question she hadn't gotten an opportunity to ask him.

In fact, it wouldn't occur to her for some time to wonder again just who had come up with a risky plan to set a trap for an elusive thief.

As good as his word, Jared pointed out a few sights on the drive to the museum. His casual, companionable attitude seemed less strained, as though he had leashed his impatience more firmly than Danica had ever known him to do before. She didn't know what that meant, but the immediate effect on her was a lessening of her wariness—something she recognized only belatedly.

A *very* dangerous man.

By the time they reached the San Francisco Museum of Historical Art, where the Bannister collection would soon be housed, Jared had also mentioned two of the people she was going to meet today. Offering more than just names, he also added brief explanations that Morgan either didn't know or else had decided to keep to herself.

As Jared pulled the car to the curb in front of the museum, Danica said, "Let me get this straight. Storm Tremaine, apparently a computer technician for Ace Security, is actually a technical specialist for Interpol? And she's engaged to Wolfe Nickerson, who happens to be the security expert and representative of Lloyd's of London?"

"That's right."

"Isn't this entire situation getting awfully tangled?"

"I think so." His voice was dry. "In fact, I'll be pleasantly surprised if the roof doesn't cave in on all of us. By the way, I don't think Morgan knows that Storm really works for me. I'm not sure, mind you, but I don't think so."

Danica didn't respond until he had gotten out and come around to open her door. As she slid from the car and watched him close the door, she murmured, "I think it'll be safer if I just pretend ignorance about everything except why *I'm* here. That seems to be the only thing that is what it appears to be."

"You may be right." Jared took her arm and guided her across the pavement toward the front doors of the museum. "I can't recall—you aren't allergic to cats, are you?"

"No. Why?"

"Storm has one. Or Bear has her; I've never been quite sure on that point."

"Bear?"

"What else could you expect from a woman named Storm? She has a little blond cat named Bear."

"And though she appears to work for Ace Security, she actually works for you and Interpol, and she's engaged to Wolfe, who works for Lloyd's of London and happens to be Max Bannister's half brother. . . ."

"You appear to find that surprising," Jared murmured.

"Not at all. Every job I take on is filled with tangled relationships, risky undercurrents, and things that aren't what they seem to be." Danica looked at the huge red banner fluttering near the front door that proclaimed the forthcoming *Mysteries Past* exhibit, then sighed and glanced up at Jared.

He met her gaze, his own warmly amused. "Yeah, I know," he said in understanding. "This whole thing has all the potential to turn into a real mess. That's what I keep telling Max."

"To which he replies . . . ?"

"That he gave his word. He's hidebound about keeping his promises. So I work on an ulcer and gray hair while Max calmly packs his priceless collection in wooden crates labeled 'knicknacks' and trucks it across the city under the noses of thieves who'd sell their miserable souls *and* commit wholesale murder to have it."

Danica couldn't help smiling at the faint note of indignation in his voice. "You would have preferred an armored truck?"

"At the very least." Then he shrugged and smiled at her. "But I should have known Max knew what he was doing. Now, if we can only stay one jump ahead of all the thieves, we might actually be able to catch one."

"According to Morgan, you've already caught a few. Even a whole gang of them just last week."

"We got lucky is what we did," Jared said with a touch of disgust as they waited for a moment beside the museum's doors for a stream of schoolchildren and their harried teacher to leave the building. "So far, we've been caught off guard more times than I like to think about. It hasn't cost us yet, but with the collection out of the vaults now . . ."

Danica knew that part of his worry was for her, because it was entirely possible that she could be viewed as a tool or a hostage or some other means of getting to the collection. But she had spent her life working with extremely valuable, often priceless gems, and she had learned long ago to accept the risk without undue anxiety; she controlled what she could and did her job, trusting that others would do theirs.

So she was able to respond serenely to Jared's concern now. "You've done everything humanly possible to protect the collection. Besides, when it comes right down to it, your job is to catch a thief."

"That's what Max says. But I'd never forgive myself if I made a mistake that cost him his collection."

Danica didn't reply to that since they entered the museum just then, but she didn't forget what she'd heard. It was something that hadn't been a part of his personality ten years ago, this willingness to admit that a mistake was possible; as a very young cop, his self-confidence where his job was concerned had bordered on arrogance.

It reminded her that just as she had been changed by experiences and the passing of time, Jared had certainly been changed as well. She couldn't go on tormenting herself by remembering all the pain of ten years ago, all the mistakes they had each made, because those two people were largely different now. This mixture of knowledge and ignorance was strange, a bit unsettling, and yet to Danica it represented her first silent admission that there might actually be a chance they could put the past behind them.

If she had the courage to try.

FOUR

It was almost an hour later when Jared began to show Danica around the museum, and she was still sorting out her various impressions of the people she had met.

Storm Tremaine, tiny and blond, with fierce eyes and a lazy Southern drawl, didn't look anything at all like a cop—or even a technical specialist. But it was clear she was small only in physical stature, not ability or self-confidence. Danica thought the computer expert, who seemed none the worse for wear after her brush with a maniac the previous week, was unusually intelligent, unflappable, quite probably fearless—and definitely in love with Wolfe Nickerson.

Wolfe surprised Danica somehow, though she couldn't have said why. He was about six feet tall and powerfully built, with somewhat shaggy auburn hair and very sharp blue eyes; those eyes literally smoldered whenever they rested on Storm—which was often—but successfully hid his thoughts the rest of the time. Even so, Danica thought there was an undercurrent of strain between him and Jared, which wasn't surprising considering that Jared was trying to catch a thief by using as bait the collection Wolfe was responsible for protecting.

Danica also sensed that Morgan was a bit guarded with both men despite her cheerful air and easy smiles, which rather reinforced the idea that she believed they posed a threat to the mysterious Quinn.

As she walked beside Jared down one of the first-floor corridors of the museum, Danica asked, "Does Morgan know about the trap?"

"I hope not," Jared replied immediately. "Too many people know already. Max hasn't told her, but he thinks she either knows or else has a hunch there's something going on. He's probably right. If she *does* know, she's being uncharacteristically quiet about it."

Mildly Danica said, "Maybe because none of you have confided in her."

"Maybe." Jared hesitated, then added, "Did she tell you about meeting Quinn a few weeks ago?"

"Yes." The way he'd put it, Danica doubted that Jared knew about the more recent meeting, and even though she felt a pang of guilt for not mentioning it, she remained silent; it was up to Morgan whom she chose to tell, after all.

Jared didn't mention Morgan again, but instead said somewhat dryly, "Maybe I should ask if you've encountered Quinn at some point in your career."

"I haven't. The closest I ever came was about a year and a half ago. I was on my way to appraise an emerald necklace in London, and Quinn apparently got there first. At least, he got the blame for the robbery."

"Let me guess. The necklace vanished in a puff of smoke?"

Danica couldn't help but smile at his sarcasm. "The press does tend to make Quinn sound like a magician, don't they? Or supernatural in some way. As if some of the reporters actually believe no human could do what he does."

"Sleight of hand, a certain amount of skill, and pure luck," Jared said in the tone of a critique. "He's human enough."

She looked up at her companion curiously. "He doesn't impress you."

Jared took her arm lightly and guided her into the south wing of the ground floor, where most of the museum's existing gem collections were housed. She thought he wasn't going to answer, but then, as they halted by a display case filled with various figurines, he finally did.

"As a matter of fact, he impresses me quite a lot— but not for the same reasons he fascinates the press and the public."

Taking a guess, Danica said, "Because you have a clearer idea of the real skill involved in his robberies?"

"Something like that." Jared looked down at her and smiled. "Why are we talking about a cat burglar?"

"You brought him up," she reminded. "I just asked if Morgan knew about the trap."

"Well, let's talk about something else."

"Fine with me."

Jared chose the most unthreatening topic he could have, and since Danica found the museum's gem collection interesting professionally as well as personally, she was able to hold up her end of the conversation as he showed her through the wing. In fact, he was so successful at maintaining a casual and companionable air between them that Danica was more startled than anything else when he abruptly pulled her into a shadowy corner more than an hour later.

"What—"

"Shhhh," Jared warned, his voice no more than a whisper. Both his hands were holding her shoulders, tense but not painfully tight, and his body half shielded hers so that she could only just see past him.

They were in a large room, open to the main corridor, which featured jewelry and which had been deserted of visitors except for them. Since the display cases were specially lighted to show the gems to advantage, and the room was somewhat dim otherwise, the dark corner he'd chosen quite effectively hid them from all but the most intent scrutiny of anyone passing through the corridor.

The two men who walked past the jewelry room a moment later were talking quietly, and neither spared more than a casual glance into the room as they passed. Danica got a good look at both of them, however. One was Kenneth Dugan, this museum's curator, whose faintly harassed air couldn't hide his intelligence or his ambition; the other was a very handsome man somewhere in his forties who was lean but sinewy and who moved with a kind of indolent grace.

When the sounds of their footsteps had vanished, Jared said a bit absently, "Sorry, but I didn't want him to see you."

Since she had met Ken Dugan along with the others earlier, Danica knew it was the second man Jared had been concerned about. "Leo Cassady?"

Jared looked down at her. "Then he would have recognized you?"

"I imagine so, since I appraised a diamond bracelet for him about four months ago. But surely you don't think he's a threat? I mean—"

"Do I mistrust Leo Cassady? No, not especially. In fact, he's a good friend of Max's. But he's a collector, which puts him on the list of people with an unusually strong interest in the Bannister collection. I'd rather not make any exceptions, for the sake of security, if nothing else. Dani, except for the people directly involved with the exhibit, I would very much rather keep you under wraps until the collection is installed here. I think it'll be safer."

Danica didn't respond immediately, but not because she was upset by his caution; it made perfect sense in terms of security precautions. She was silent because while he had been explaining, she'd become aware of how close they were. Of how dim this shadowy corner was. And of how alone they were here. She couldn't seem to take her eyes off his face.

Odd. Even in this low light, his striking eyes were distinct. She thought she would know him even in total darkness, anywhere at all. No wonder she had never been able to forget him, she admitted silently.

"Dani . . ." His voice was low, husky, and his fingers tightened on her shoulders. "Don't look at me like that."

"Like what?" she murmured, realizing only then that he could see her more clearly because of their positions.

He seemed to catch his breath. "Like you want me."

Danica's common sense warned her that she should look away, step back—anything to break the connection between them. But despite the fact that she was the one who kept saying they needed to take things slowly, the warning went unheard. She felt caught up in something she didn't want to struggle against, and it didn't matter to her that they were standing in a room of a public museum, where the likelihood of being interrupted was quite high.

Jared lifted one hand from her shoulder to touch her face, tilting it up a bit more, the rough pad of his thumb rubbing across her lower lip slowly. "You could always drive me crazy with just a look," he told her in that same low, raspy voice. "Those big eyes, dark and gleaming, so deep they seemed bottomless. Just one look, and I could barely remember my name. I wanted to slay dragons for you, did you know that, Dani?"

"No," she whispered, her lips throbbing from the sensual little caress, her heartbeat quickening.

"I did. Maybe that was why . . ."

Maybe that was why he'd fought so fiercely with her father, Danica finished, but silently. After all, the only dragon he could have imagined near her had been her father. If so, it must have been even more devastating for him to have lost the battle.

"There aren't any dragons," she told him, her voice still hardly more than a whisper. "Just people—good or bad, right or wrong."

His thumb was rubbing her bottom lip rhythmically, his shadowed face very still. He didn't say anything, but when one of her hands lifted to rest on his chest, the movement seemed to snap whatever restraint he'd been holding on to. He bent his head suddenly and covered her mouth with his.

It was what Danica wanted, what she'd invited, and she didn't try to deceive herself about it. She felt his hand slide under her hair to the nape of her neck, felt his other hand move down her back to her hips, and her body molded itself to his instantly. This time the strength of her own response to him didn't shock Danica, but it wouldn't have mattered even then; her body knew what it wanted.

Though the first touch of his mouth was light, Jared deepened the kiss almost at once, accepting the invitation of her parting lips with a hunger he made no effort to hide. It was a kind of possession, that kiss, hard and hot, achingly seductive and more than a little bit wild, and Danica responded with a matching intensity.

She slid her arms underneath his open suit jacket and around his waist, vaguely taking note of the gun he wore in a shoulder holster when her hand brushed it, but not unduly disturbed by the weapon; it was another indication of security to which her job had made her accustomed. She just wanted to be closer to him, and felt frustrated by their clothing. But even with the barriers, the heat and hardness of his body seduced hers, making her breasts swell and ache, her legs tremble, and her heart pound wildly against her ribs.

He made a rough sound when he released her mouth at last, and his hooded eyes gleamed at her briefly before he began exploring her throat. Her head fell back to allow him more room, her fingers clutched at his back, and Danica had the vague idea that she would have collapsed in a heap on the cold marble floor if he hadn't been holding her so tightly.

She couldn't breathe very well, but it didn't seem to matter with his mouth moving over her flesh and his hard body pressed against hers. Then, as her dazed eyes finally focused on her surroundings, she remembered where they were, and a little sound of disappointment escaped her.

Jared lifted his head, staring down at her. His breathing was uneven, and he had to clear his throat before he could speak. "Did I hurt you?"

Danica shook her head a little, realizing as she did so that he had misunderstood her murmur of disappointment. "No . . . no. But this isn't a very good place to . . . I mean—"

He kissed her, briefly but by no means lightly, then pulled away with obvious reluctance. "I know, I know. Too damned public, and hardly comfortable." His voice was still a bit rough.

She forced her arms to release him, struggling to regain her own calm. It was unexpectedly difficult, with her entire body still aching with desire for him, but her mind was clouded with sudden anxiety and that gave her some willpower. She couldn't blame him this time for trying to sweep her off her feet; her own desire had been the spark between them and he had more or less warned her what her hungry gaze was risking. But that didn't change the fact that she still felt rushed, carried along by a force beyond her control—and it was frightening.

"Dani?"

She felt his hands gripping her shoulders, and met his intense gaze hesitantly. But before she could try to find the words to explain her feelings to him, another voice intruded.

"Jared? Oh, good, I thought I'd never find—oh. I think this is what they call a case of rotten timing. I'll just go away and come back later, okay?"

Jared muttered a curse under his breath, but when he released Danica and turned to face Morgan, his face was calm. "Never mind. You were looking for me, obviously. What's up?"

Holding her usual clipboard in front of her as if she feared she might need a shield, Morgan said, "Sorry, but Storm and Wolfe sent me to find you. They need you in the computer room. Some kind of question about security, I gather." She smiled brightly. "I thought I'd show Dani the exhibit's wing while you go take care of business. I mean, since you two obviously haven't made it past the ground floor . . ."

In spite of her inner turmoil, Danica had to smile at the other woman's gentle mockery, but she bent her head so Jared wouldn't see her amusement.

Somewhat shortly Jared said to Morgan, "I saw Ken pass by here a few minutes ago; is he still in the museum?"

"You must have lost track of time—Ken and Leo

left quite a while ago. And the museum's closing. It's almost six."

"Dani?"

"Hmmm?" she murmured without looking up.

"I'll catch up with you later, all right?"

She nodded. "That's fine."

"You won't leave without me?"

Danica did look up at him then, surprised by the abrupt, curiously taut question. "No, of course not."

He seemed to relax. "Good." Without another word, he strode past Morgan and left the room.

"Whew." Morgan took a hesitant step forward. "There goes a truly unhappy man. I really *am* sorry, Dani."

Danica came out of the shadowy corner slowly, still coping with legs that were unsteady and a pulse that refused to settle down to a normal rhythm. The man's effect on her was nothing short of astonishing. "It's all right. We were just . . . discussing how inappropriate a museum could be."

Morgan nodded gravely. "Never the time and the place, as a poet once remarked. But I didn't help things by barging in, I'm sure."

"You're forgiven."

"Not by Jared—but I never expect impossible things." Morgan chuckled. "Anyway, like I said, I thought this might be a good time for me to show you where Max's collection is going to be exhibited."

Danica welcomed the suggestion, largely because

she wanted to occupy her mind with something unthreatening. So, with an "after you" gesture and smile at the other woman, she followed Morgan out of the jewelry room.

"What I don't understand," Storm drawled somewhat absently as she typed commands into the computer, "is why you're still snapping at Jared. He's just doing his job."

Resting a hip on the corner of her desk and wearing her little blond cat on his shoulder, Wolfe was waiting for his lady to finish the work she insisted had to be completed today. Jared had left the room only moments before, and though a security problem had been ironed out successfully, neither man had been happy with the other.

"He nearly got you killed," Wolfe muttered, reaching up absently to scratch Bear under his chin. "Besides that, I don't like being lied to."

Eyeing him shrewdly, Storm said, "You haven't been snapping at Max—or me. Neither of us was especially truthful there for a while. Give Jared a break, will you, please?"

"I *am* giving him a break. I'm still speaking to him."

Storm laughed softly, shaking her head. If she had learned anything since meeting him, it was that Wolfe's stubbornness equaled her own. "Well, just try to remember that he *is* on our side, after all. He's not the enemy."

"All right."

She sat back in her chair as the computer digested her commands, and smiled up at him. "Besides, there are better ways to focus your energy. Do you realize you haven't thrown me to the floor and had your way with me even once today?"

He frowned. "Wasn't that you this morning? Among all the boxes in the living room?"

"Yes, but that was before breakfast."

He leaned across the desk, meeting her halfway as she straightened in her chair, and kissed her. "And wasn't that you I had lunch with today?" he murmured.

"Yes, but that was in a bed."

Wolfe glanced aside at the minuscule floor space of the computer room, then eyed her rather cluttered desk. "Well, there's no room in here."

Storm sighed mournfully. "I knew it. Engaged barely a week, and already you're getting bored with me."

"If I get any more bored with you, they're going to have to put me in traction."

She laughed. "Complaining?"

"Hell, no." He smiled, and his eyes were like the glowing blue at the base of a flame. "In fact, I'm a bit anxious to get back to that new house of ours and have another go at christening the bed."

They had found and leased a terrific house with an enclosed garden where Bear could sun himself and chase bugs, and had moved their things there days ago. But with their working hours—and tendency to forget practical matters whenever they were alone—they were still in the process of settling in.

Though they hadn't yet decided where "home" would be in the future, the *Mysteries Past* exhibit would demand both of them to remain in San Francisco for at least the coming months.

"We need to finish unpacking," she pointed out mildly.

"A minute ago you were hot for my body," he said in a wounded tone.

"I still am, but when it comes to love among the boxes—once is enough." Storm grinned at him and began typing in the commands that would get her out of the computer system for the day. "By the way, even though neither of you has said much about it, it's pretty obvious you and Jared have known each other for years. Not so surprising, I suppose, given your jobs. Did you know he used to be married?"

Wolfe sat up straighter, startled. "No, I didn't."

She nodded, still casual. "I heard about it when I first started working with him. But not from him, of course; somebody else in the office. It was years ago, and a very brief marriage, but my source said he was never the same after the divorce. Seems he was absolutely crazy about her."

"Then why the divorce?"

"You'll have to ask him. Or her."

"Her?"

Storm shut the computer down and got to her feet. "Umm. An expert gemologist with an unusual name. I doubt there are two of them. Danica."

After a moment, Wolfe shook his head. "Is fate taking a hand, or did we tangle this situation on our own?"

"I think we're doing a pretty good job of it on our own." She smiled a bit wryly as she went around the desk to join him. "But it's another reason why you shouldn't waste your energy staying mad at Jared. We'll need our full concentration just to keep all the players straight."

Wolfe had to admit—she was right.

After Jared returned to Danica, they didn't say very much to each other, either at the museum or, later, at the restaurant where he took her for dinner. Since the interlude in the museum, neither had been able to recapture the earlier mood of casual companionship, and as Jared watched Danica open the door to her temporary apartment, the strain was beginning to show in them both.

"May I come in?" Jared asked.

Out of sheer self-preservation, Danica wanted to refuse him now. She was still feeling both confused and a little frightened by the strength of her own desire, and she needed some time alone to try to sort through her emotions.

In a very quiet, even voice, Jared said, "Dani, there are two video cameras in this foyer that are constantly monitored by one of the security guards downstairs. Either let me come in, or else tell me to get lost—but let's not stand here like waxworks entertaining him."

Silently she stepped back and allowed him in. She closed the door behind him and led the way into the living room. She'd left a couple of lamps burning, but like the evening before, the room was mostly lit by the reddish glow of the setting sun.

"I forgot about the cameras," she murmured. "Sorry."

"No, I'm sorry." He sounded impatient now. "I'm sorry you have to live under such close scrutiny."

Danica was faintly surprised. "I've done it before, you know that. It's part of the job." She shrugged. "Would you like a drink? Coffee?" Keep it casual . . . keep it light, she told herself.

He shook his head. He was standing near the northwest corner of the room, so that the sunlight spilled in behind and around him, giving him a sort of aura.

He looked dangerous, she thought, even though she couldn't see his face very clearly. He was still, and the reddish glow of his silhouette was heated and ominous. Like a sign or a warning. The tension between them was so strong that Danica could feel it in the air like something with a life of its own. She kept remembering the museum and the hunger for him that had filled her body and clouded her mind, and she didn't know what to say to him now.

Abruptly he took three long steps to stand before her, the sunlight aura disappearing. His face was taut, his eyes darkened. "Do you realize you've hardly spoken to me since what happened in the museum?" he asked tensely.

Danica folded her arms beneath her breasts, half-conscious of the warning implied by her body language, but so trapped by his gaze, she knew it hardly mattered; there was no warning him off, not when her own will-power was so puny.

"You . . . haven't said much yourself," she managed.

His hands lifted to catch her shoulders, fingers flexing restlessly. "I know. I was afraid—I didn't know how you were feeling about me. It nearly got out of control at the museum, and I was afraid I might have pushed too hard."

It wasn't easy for Danica to swallow her pride, and the reluctance of that was audible in her low voice. "You didn't push. You didn't do anything I . . . I didn't want you to do."

His eyes narrowed slightly and the fingers on her shoulders tightened, but his voice was quiet. "Is that why you're upset? Because you wanted me?"

She shook her head a little helplessly, oddly embarrassed by his last question despite—or perhaps because of—her former intimacy with this man. "I don't know. Maybe. It's . . . too fast, too sudden. I know it was my fault, what happened, because you were taking things slowly the way I asked—"

"Don't talk about fault, Dani, as if you did something wrong," he said, his voice husky now. "The way you looked at me, the way you wanted me, could never be wrong, no matter what."

Ensnared by him, pulled toward him even though he didn't move, Danica fought against the almost overwhelming urge to give in and allow herself to be swept along mindlessly. It was actually painful to resist; her entire body ached and she felt as if a fever burned inside her.

Trying to hold her voice steady, she said, "I don't know if it was wrong for *me*, that's what scares me. I can't—I don't know how to control it."

"Dani—"

"Wait, hear me out, please. You said yourself how . . . how much Dad controlled me all those years. He did. I loved him, but I can't deny that. He controlled my life for so long, I hardly said a word or made a move that wasn't governed by him. When he was killed, I . . ."

Jared squeezed her shoulders gently when her voice trailed off. "You were lost?"

Relieved that he understood that much, she nodded, and his sensitivity enabled her to be more candid about it than she might otherwise have been. "It was terrifying. For the first time in my life, I was alone. I had to make choices, decisions that had always been made for me. Until then, the only important thing I'd ever decided was to marry you, and even in that . . ."

"Even in that," Jared finished slowly, "you were never given a chance to think it through. It was less your decision than mine. Because I was so sure, and so impatient to have you."

Danica drew a shaky breath, still fighting the urge to throw herself into his arms. She wished he wasn't touching her, yet didn't want him to stop. "I had to learn to think for myself after Dad died, and it was hard. So hard that when I finally gained control of my life, I knew I'd never want to give that up. I don't ever want to be a pawn again, not to anyone or anything."

"I don't much like that word," he said, tense now, "but I'll use it too. Pawns are sacrificed, used to achieve an end and then discarded after they've served their purpose. Is that what you're afraid of with me, Dani? That I'll use you and then throw you away?"

"No, not that . . . I don't believe you're that cruel or ruthless."

"Thank you for that, at least." The glitter of anger in his eyes died, and he shook his head slightly. "You said this was happening too fast, then you talked about control and pawns; what is it you're afraid of? I can't deal with the problem until I know what it is."

She knew how jumbled it all must sound to him, but the confusion reflected her state of mind. Trying to keep it relatively simple and clear, she said, "I feel . . . rushed, pulled at . . . overwhelmed. I know you're trying to take things slowly, I *know* that, but it doesn't seem to matter. Whatever this is, what you make me feel when you're near me, when you touch me, I can't control it. I try to, but—"

Jared looked down at her for a long moment, an odd light in his eyes that she didn't understand. Then he smiled slightly and stepped back, releasing her. "All right."

Danica was puzzled by his response, and a little wary. "All right, what?"

"All right, you go on trying to control what you feel. I'll go on being as patient as I know how to be. We'll give ourselves a little more time. Agreed?"

She wished he hadn't taken his hands from her shoulders; they felt cold now. And she had the peculiar feeling that some turning point had been reached without her awareness. In any case, there was only one answer she could give him. "Agreed," she said in a carefully composed voice.

"Good. How about lunch tomorrow?"

"I need to work."

"You have to break for meals. Look, I'll make it easier—I'll get takeout, and we can eat here. That way your work won't be interrupted for very long. I promise to leave right after the meal so I won't be a pest."

He sounded so reasonable, it made her vaguely suspicious. "All right. I mean—thank you, that sounds fine."

His lips twitched a bit when she remembered her manners, but he didn't comment. "Do you like Chinese?"

"Yes, very much."

"Then that's what I'll bring. I'll see you tomorrow, Dani, about one."

She nodded and watched him move across the room toward the door. She wanted to run after him, call him back. Shake him. Was it her imagination, she wondered, or had he been more pleased than anything else about her confusion? Jared paused just before he left the room and looked back at her. He was still smiling slightly, and his voice was calm when he spoke.

"We all think we have control over our lives, but it's only an illusion, you know."

She nodded slightly. "I know we can't control everything. But I control what I can."

It was his turn to nod, slowly and thoughtfully. His voice didn't change when he said, "Not a bad philosophy—if you can accept a basic truth."

"Which is?"

"Nobody masters love, Dani. Nobody. It masters us. That's the nature of the beast."

She didn't say another word, gazing after him as he left the apartment. Oddly the last of the reddish sunlight vanished from the room even as he did.

Love?

It couldn't have happened again, could it? With all the pain between them, all the regrets and mistakes, surely she couldn't have fallen in love with him again. . . .

Danica went to a chair almost blindly and sank down into it. Was that why she felt so out of control? Why her entire body ached and throbbed so incessantly and why she couldn't seem to heed her own mind's sensible warnings to keep Jared at arm's length? Was her almost desperate fear of losing control quite simply a fear of losing herself in him a second time?

Nobody masters love. Nobody.

Had it been so obvious to him? At seventeen, she had been unable to hide her feelings; was she no better at twenty-eight? Was he sure, as he had been before, that she was his for the taking? She thought he probably was; there had been something of triumph in his smile.

The question was . . . was he right?

It was nearly midnight, and Jared stood restlessly at the window of his hotel room. His suit jacket and tie had long since been discarded, but he still wore his big automatic in its accustomed shoulder holster, and he only needed to pull on a light jacket if he had to leave in a hurry. Which is what he more or less expected.

It was an unusually clear night, affording an excellent view of the colorful city lights, but he wasn't interested. He had, with enormous difficulty, managed to keep his mind off Danica and on what he had come here to do, but only because his work demanded all the caution of walking a knife's edge and he had taught himself long ago to focus his concentration. Too often, keeping his mind on business had been a simple matter of life or death.

When the phone finally rang, he turned instantly from the window and picked up the receiver. "Hello?"

"I hear things are a little tense between you and Wolfe."

Jared relaxed, but only slightly. "And have you also heard that Morgan talks too much?"

"Yes, I have heard that—but how do you know it was Morgan? It might have been Storm."

"I know Storm. She'll talk to Wolfe about me, but she wouldn't talk to you, Max, not about undercurrents."

Max chuckled. "No, you trained her too well. As a matter of fact, it was Morgan who mentioned the strain."

"Yeah, well—give her two points for observation; it didn't take ESP to see it."

"You want me to talk to him?"

"No, I don't think so." Jared was glancing at his watch as he spoke. "Between his preoccupation with

Storm and his hostility toward me, he hasn't had a lot of time to think about what we're doing, and I'd just as soon keep it that way as long as possible. The last thing I want right now is a lot of questions."

Max was silent for a moment, then sighed. "All right, I'll keep out of it. For now."

"Thanks."

"Don't mention it. I would like a favor in return, though."

"Name it."

"Bring Danica to our apartment tomorrow night for dinner. Dinah wants to meet her."

Jared didn't respond for a moment, then asked a somewhat grim question. "Just what else did Morgan have to tell you? Dammit, Max, is she your spy?"

Chuckling, Max said, "I've never heard you sound so paranoid before."

"Answer the question."

"No, she isn't my spy. In fact, she didn't mention anything about you two beyond the fact that you were at the museum today. Nobody had to tell me, Jared. You forget—I saw your face yesterday after you talked to her. You might have divorced Danica, but you didn't leave her in the past."

"Give yourself a few points for observation," Jared said with forced lightness, tacitly admitting the truth of Max's statement. "Look, I'll ask Dani about dinner and let you know tomorrow, all right?"

"Fine. And relax, will you?" Amusement crept into

Max's deep voice. "As tense as you are, anybody'd think there was something dangerous going on."

Jared made a rude noise and cradled the receiver without force. His somewhat rueful amusement didn't last long, however. He checked his watch and remained by the phone for some minutes, but when it finally rang, it pulled him away from the window for a second time.

And this time the conversation was much briefer.

"Yeah?"

"You sound impatient. Am I late?"

Jared checked his watch again. "Yes. I was about to go looking for you."

"You wouldn't have found me."

"Don't bet on it."

A soft laugh. "One of these days, we'll put that to the test, you and I."

"If we live long enough, you're on. Now, do we need to meet tonight?"

"I think so. . . ."

FIVE

During the next week, Danica had reason to be thankful for one of her father's teachings. He had, in the years after her divorce from Jared, drummed it into her that the better she was at hiding her feelings, the less likely it was that she would find herself betrayed by them. That coupled with his annoyance at restless movements in his presence had taught her well to hold her expression calm and not to fidget.

That manufactured cloak of serenity was something she wrapped tightly around herself as the days passed. She concentrated fiercely on her work, cleaning and appraising the fabulous pieces of the Bannister collection one by one—and during the time she spent with Jared she held on to calm, detached composure with both hands.

At first, Jared's behavior helped her. He was completely casual and friendly without even a hint of intimacy. He brought Chinese takeout to the apartment the day after their museum trip and kept up a light conversation, never once referring to the previous day. He left promptly after the meal, pausing only to extend Max's invitation and to agree on what time he'd pick her up that evening.

The dinner was pleasant, and Danica certainly enjoyed meeting Max's delicate wife, finding the redheaded Dinah to be as friendly and intelligent as she was beautiful. Max, obviously deeply in love with his wife, was his usual calm and kind self and a perfect host; if he saw or sensed any conflict in his guests, he gave no sign.

As for Jared, he was low-key and agreeable, the intensity she had come to expect in him completely hidden. Other than taking her arm when they walked, he didn't touch her, and left her at her apartment door with a pleasant good night.

For the first few days, Danica was grateful for the complete lack of pressure from him. It gave her time to try to understand her own feelings and motivations, and their easygoing conversations explored their likes and dislikes with a thoroughness that had been completely missing all those years ago.

She was able to concentrate and worked during the day, usually breaking for lunch outside the apartment— mostly with Jared, though twice it was Morgan who was her companion. Jared took her out in the evening four times during that first week, dinner followed by a movie or concert where the crowds were heavy and she was unlikely to be seen and recognized by anyone interested in priceless gems.

Each time, Danica found herself delivered back to her door with no more than friendly courtesy. She impulsively invited him in for coffee or a drink late one night, only to have the invitation politely refused. He had seemed a bit preoccupied and distant, his refusal almost absentminded, and the seeming indifference didn't help her efforts to understand her own feelings—far less his.

The nights were long, and though Danica was generally untroubled by insomnia, she had difficulty now and woke often, tossing and turning, feeling hot and restless and unable to go back to sleep with her usual ease. The dreams she remembered were so erotic they shocked her, and more than once she actually got out of bed in the middle of the night for a cool shower to soothe her feverish body.

Her cloak of serenity very soon became thread-bare.

She found herself in the somewhat bewildering position of having been given exactly what she wanted—the time to think and no overwhelming intensity from him—only to find it far more frustrating than beneficial. She had also come to the conclusion that her lack of experience in the romantic arena was a definite drawback; she had no idea if Jared was merely following her wishes or if he had simply lost interest in her.

It was the latter possibility that forced her to make a decision. She had to know if he still wanted her, the uncertainty was tormenting her. She knew she was risking herself no matter what his answer turned out to be; by showing him the question was important to her, she was making herself vulnerable to him. But she had no choice.

So, when he issued one of his casual dinner invitations halfway through her second week in San Francisco, Danica just as casually said she was in the mood to make spaghetti if he didn't mind eating in. She wouldn't have been very surprised if he had refused, but she startled herself by feeling physically weak with relief when he promptly accepted.

Lord, *was* it that important to her?

She considered the question early that evening as she stirred up a spicy sauce and assembled the ingredients for a salad before Jared arrived. He had told her that no one mastered love, then had withdrawn emotionally so that she was left facing her confusion alone. Wisdom? Tactics? Or mere indifference? Whichever had been his motivation, the result was that she had been forced to admit the truth to herself.

It was a terrifying truth. Even with absolutely no pressure from him, she had no hope of controlling—of mastering—her feelings for him. She shied away from calling it love; having given her heart to him once and paying the price for that vulnerability, she was far more guarded now. She couldn't deny the strong emotions she felt, but desire and passion seemed . . . less all-consuming. Less threatening to her peace. But whatever label her feelings should have been given, they were too powerful to be ignored.

They had grown stronger and stronger as the days passed, surging inside her like a tide, filling her until there was nothing else that mattered to her. Despite his seeming disinterest, she had caught herself staring at him and fought a constant urge to touch him whenever they were together, and her heartbeat quickened at the first sound of his voice.

She was still wary of being swept up helplessly in anything, and that was the strongest reason why she had chosen to confront Jared and learn the truth of his feelings in spite of the risk; it gave her some sense of remaining in control of her fate.

That was what she told herself as she worked efficiently in the kitchen. That was what she told herself as she drew the threadbare serenity around her for whatever protection it might offer. And that was what she told herself when she went to let Jared in a little after seven.

She had dressed with deliberate casualness in a long red cowl-necked sweater over snug black pants, an outfit in which she felt comfortable and about which he made no comment. Not that she had expected him to, of course, even though she had always been told that red was definitely her color.

He had brought the wine, and didn't waste any

time tossing his suit jacket over the back of the couch and loosening his tie. Danica eyed the gun he wore as habitually as most men wore a watch.

Mildly she said, "It's interesting to have armed dinner guests. But I meant to ask you before this—since you're out of your jurisdiction, technically speaking, weren't you supposed to leave that gun in Paris?"

Jared looked down at the shoulder holster, grimaced slightly, and began unfastening it. "Sorry. I'm so used to it, sometimes I forget." He shrugged off the holster and placed it over his jacket.

"You didn't answer my question."

"You're right. Technically speaking I shouldn't carry a gun here, especially since the San Francisco police have no official knowledge of what I'm doing in their fair city."

"How about unofficial knowledge?" she asked as she led the way into the kitchen.

Jared followed, rolling up the sleeves of his white shirt. "Not much of that either, I'm afraid. Max asked the police commissioner for a favor, and since nobody refuses Max Bannister, I have special permission to carry—and use—a gun. Other than the commissioner, only one cop in the city knows what I'm doing here. Inspector Keane Tyler. Remind me to leave you his number just in case. I should have done it before now."

Danica stirred the bubbling sauce and began heating water for the spaghetti to give herself a moment before she responded. In spite of her knowledge about his job, the potential danger was something she hadn't thought much about—not when they had been married in the past and not in the present. But his casual words about Inspector Tyler's knowledge of his activities was sobering, even chilling.

He was setting a trap for a criminal, which, all by itself, was dangerous enough. But he was also playing something of a lone hand, working "unofficially" and without the support of his Paris office or the local police—and that multiplied the danger. He was risking his life, she thought. And he could lose.

"Of course, Max is the one you should call if anything goes wrong and you can't reach me," he went on in the same unruffled voice. "Consider Tyler a backup. I hope there's a corkscrew in this place."

"That drawer," she answered automatically, pointing. "And glasses in the cabinet over the dishwasher."

He found both and worked briskly to uncork the wine. "What can I do to help?" he asked her.

Surprised, she said, "I don't think of you as handy in a kitchen. You weren't before."

"I was an arrogant ass before," he said, pouring the wine into two delicate goblets. When Danica didn't respond immediately, he looked at her with a slight smile and amusement in his eyes. "You might at least pretend to disagree."

She found herself smiling back at him, feeling both pleasure and slight confusion at his teasing. This was an entirely different mood from the detachment she had grown accustomed to, and she wasn't quite sure how to react.

"A good hostess never disagrees with her guest," she murmured. "However, if you really do want to help, you can fix the salad. Everything's there by the sink."

Jared handed her a goblet of wine with a slight bow. "My pleasure, ma'am. And just for your information, I happen to be a pretty fair cook now. It makes living alone a bit more bearable."

"How are you at cleaning up after?"

"Not so enthusiastic, but willing. If I've learned anything, it's that there's nothing wise about leaving a mess for somebody else to deal with."

Danica knew he wasn't just talking about dirty kitchens, but she didn't probe. She was already so unnerved by her realization of potential danger to him that delving into another bleak topic was something she resisted. Instead she busied herself at the stove while he began preparing the salad, and they worked companionably together.

Their conversation remained casual all during the meal, and it wasn't until the table had been cleared, the dishwasher loaded, and they took their coffee into the living room that Danica's tension really grew. The drapes were drawn against the twilight outside, shutting the rest of the world away from them, so that they were very alone. It was only then that it occurred to her how difficult it was going to be for her to do what she had decided to do. How could she ask him about his feelings, his intentions? What could she say to him?

Do you still want me? Because, if you don't, please tell me now while I still have a chance of surviving it. . . .

"Dani?"

Sitting on the couch only a foot or so away from him, she leaned forward to set her cup on the coffee table beside his. What could she say? She settled back into her corner with her hands folded in her lap and looked at him, hoping her feelings didn't show. She couldn't seem to think clearly, and when she did speak, the words were more or less blurted out.

"I've almost finished my work here. In a few days, the collection will be ready to be moved to the museum."

He nodded slightly, his face grave and the seawater eyes unreadable. "Max is very impressed. If you ever need a reference, he'll provide a glowing one."

She wanted to snap, *I don't give a damn about Max!* But she didn't say anything of the kind, of course. She was far too calm and controlled a woman to have a temper tantrum, at least, that was what people said.

Evenly she said, "I'm supposed to authenticate and appraise another private collection in Philadelphia next, but that's weeks away. I'll probably take some time off. Maybe go back to New York."

"Will you?" There was no emotion in his voice and none apparent in his expression; he might have been asking her the time for all the interest he showed.

As quickly as it had risen, Danica's unusual and unfamiliar anger collapsed, leaving her feeling utterly miserable and cold with pain. He couldn't care about her, she thought, not when the mention of her leaving had so little effect on him. Her gaze fell away from his calm eyes as she tried to drag her pride out of hiding.

Then she saw something that caused hope to leap inside her. She was looking at his hand where it rested on his thigh. Powerful and beautiful, it aroused heated memories of his touch and her response to it. It also told her something else. Belying his expressionless face and tranquil eyes, his hand was clenched so rigidly that the knuckles shone white through his tanned flesh.

Slowly, gazing at his hand from beneath her lashes, she murmured, "You aren't going to ask me to stay?"

"No," he said calmly, and the bones seemed to writhe under his skin as his hand clenched even tighter.

Danica looked at his face and finally understood. If she allowed the subject to drop, Jared wouldn't say one word to bring it up again. His casual manner would continue, until she waved good-bye from a plane heading east. He would let her go without a murmur of protest—not because he didn't care, but because he cared too much. Because he had focused every ounce of that incredible will of his on the determination not to make at least one of the mistakes he had made the first time.

He was making sure that Danica remained solidly on her own two feet, without pressure and without being overwhelmed by his emotions. Whatever happened between them would have to be her decision, her choice. It was a choice she had already made, but she couldn't help wondering if the cost of her vulnerability would be more than she could afford to pay.

After a long moment, she said quietly, "Even if it's what I want?"

A muscle leaped in his jaw as he clamped his teeth together, and his eyes went curiously opaque. "Is it what you want?" he asked a bit jerkily.

"That depends on you, Jared. If you've decided you don't want me anymore, then I'll go. But if you do still want me . . . I'd like to stay."

"Why? Just because I want you?"

"No. Because I want you too."

He sighed roughly, as if he'd been holding his breath, but remained still. "Are you sure, Dani?"

"About wanting you? Very sure."

His hand lifted from his thigh, the clenched fingers straightening stiffly, and touched her cheek. She turned her head until her lips pressed the rough warmth of his palm.

With a hoarse groan, he pulled her into his arms and covered her mouth with his. Danica melted against him, her arms sliding up around his neck, her lips parting eagerly beneath the hard pressure of his. Desire lanced through her with the sharp heat of pure energy, the force of it stunning.

It was far more than a simple kiss could be, she realized dazedly. It was a kind of detonation. Just like in the museum days before, he was making love to her, building her desire swiftly to a fever pitch. He wasn't detached now or indifferent, he wasn't asking for her response, and there was nothing even remotely calm about him.

"God, Dani," he muttered against her lips. His face was so taut it was masklike, and the mask was a hunger so intense it was pain.

She touched his face with trembling fingers as their breath mingled, everything inside her poised in waiting, aching for him. This was what he must have meant when he'd said she had been too young to respond to him fully when they were married, because she had no memory of feeling such an urgent need.

Her heart was pounding so hard and fast it was as if she were in the final stretch of some dreadful marathon, and it was a race she had to win to live. She couldn't say a word, yet she felt certain she would go out of her mind if he didn't make love to her right now.

Jared made a rough sound and kissed her again, the slow penetration of his tongue so erotic that Danica whimpered and closed her eyes again, drugged with hunger. Her breasts felt hot and full against his chest, aching, and she wanted to beg him to touch them with his hands, to rid her of the sweater and her bra and all the rest because the constriction of clothing was unbearable and she wanted to be naked in his arms.

She felt one of his hands slip underneath the hem of her sweater and slide up her spine, making her move to his touch in a sensuous way like the unthinking, voluptuous movement of a cat being stroked. Her breasts pressed more fully against his hard chest and she whimpered again in a pleading sound.

He muttered something she couldn't understand and for a moment held her fiercely against him, as if he wanted to merge their bodies. Then he moved, still kissing her. Clinging to him, her mouth wild under his, she felt herself gathered up and lifted off the couch. Then, almost immediately, she felt the thick carpet beneath her as she was lowered to the floor.

If she had still needed reassurance that he wanted her, that stark impatience would have provided it; he wouldn't—or couldn't—wait long enough even to get them to the bedroom. Danica didn't need the reassurance any longer, and since her need matched his, she didn't care where they were.

He leaned over her as she opened her eyes, and his voice was hardly more than a raspy whisper. "I've got to see you. . . ." He caught the hem of her sweater and tugged, pulling it off as she lifted her arms to help him and then throwing it aside.

As soon as her arms were free, she reached up to him, fumbling with the buttons of his shirt. He more or less ripped it off, his burning eyes fixed on her, and as soon as the shirt was discarded, he lowered his head to her.

She felt his mouth moving between her breasts, felt his hands slide underneath her to find the clasp of her bra, and her nails dug into his shoulders when he stripped the silk and lace away to bare her to the waist. She stared up at him when he lifted his head, and his expression as he gazed down at her sent a new, sharper desire piercing through her.

Want. Need. A hunger so intense it was like starvation, clawing wildly to be fed.

He was shaking, she could feel it. Shaking just as she was. Out of control as she was. His hand trembled when he cupped her breast, kneading and stroking, making her moan and arch into his touch. The waves of burning pleasure swept over Danica, growing ever more intense as he caressed and tormented her, and when his mouth closed hotly over her aching nipple, the sensation was so acute she could only writhe in silent pleasure and clutch at him pleadingly.

Jared was breathing heavily, his body rigid with strain, but he was too enthralled by her and her response to him to be willing to hurry the loving in spite of the savage demands of his own critical need. Her breasts, round and swollen with passion, fit his hands perfectly, the velvety pink nipples so sensitive they pulsed in his mouth. Her golden skin was heated silk, and her throaty murmurs of desire the most potent aphrodisiac he had ever known or imagined.

He had to see all of her, touch all of her. Roughly he stripped her snug pants down her legs and pulled them free of her, sending her shoes flying along with the pants. She was left with only delicate, flesh-colored panties, and the thin material tore under his impatient fingers as he disposed of them.

She was staring up at him, her dark eyes huge, liquid, bottomless. Her lips, swollen and reddened from the force of his passion, were parted and trembling, and her breath came as quickly as his. *Dear God, she was beautiful.*

He took her mouth again, stroking deeply with his tongue, enticing hers to an instant response. He caressed her breasts until she was moaning into his mouth, then slid his hand down over her quivering belly. His palm covered the soft dark curls and his fingers delved between her thighs. With a wild little sound in the back of her throat, she arched up against him, her legs parting for him jerkily.

Jared thought his heart was going to burst from his chest it pounded so violently, and it was almost more than he could bear to keep his touch slow and gentle, but the intense pleasure of arousing her so completely more than made up for the growing pain of restraint. He touched the soft feminine folds, sliding his fingers into her damp heat, finding and stroking the tiny, sensitive nubbin of flesh.

Her hips lifted to his touch, undulating instinctively, and her mouth was even wilder under his. Jared raised his head, sacrificing the pleasure of her lips for the equally profound pleasure of watching her face, hauntingly beautiful in her absorbed, urgent passion. He caressed her rhythmically, pausing for a moment to slide one finger deeply into her and groaning aloud at the exquisite heat and tightness, then withdrew slowly and resumed the rhythmic stroking.

He brought her almost to the peak, until her feverish body demanded release, then took his hands off her long enough to rid himself of his clothing. He had to be inside her, had to feel her pleasure as intimately as he could.

Danica was barely aware of what he was doing for a moment, because he'd left her trembling on the brink and her every sense was raw with the awful tension. Before she could retreat very far from that edge, he was quickly back with her, rising above her, his hips smooth against her inner thighs. She felt his body demanding entrance, hard and hot, and caught her breath raggedly at the overwhelming sensation of her body admitting him.

She had forgotten how it felt, how shockingly intimate the physical act was. Staring up at his strained face, lost in his burning eyes, she felt him come deeply into her with an exquisite slowness so erotic, she was once more quivering on the very brink of a sensual explosion. Held utterly motionless by the breathless suspension, she felt the tension gathering, coiling, and she knew she couldn't bear it a moment longer.

Almost the instant he settled fully into the cradle of her thighs, she went over the brink, crying out in surprise and triumph as wave after throbbing wave of ecstasy tore through her body. Jared made a low, guttural sound, his face tightening in a spasm of excruciating pleasure. The inner contractions of her release held him, caressed him with a pulsing touch so incredible, he thought he'd go out of his mind.

With another guttural sound, he began moving inside her, catching her pleasure before it had a chance to ebb and pushing it even higher. She whimpered and lifted her hips to meet his heavy thrusts, her legs wrapped around him, her nails digging into his back, wide, dark eyes dazed and mindless.

Each time he buried himself in the wet heat of her, Jared thought he couldn't take another second's delay, that his pounding heart would burst from his chest, but his body couldn't seem to get enough of Danica. He wanted to absorb her into himself, to merge with her until nothing could ever separate them again. It was a wild, primitive emotion, controlling his mind as surely as physical need controlled his body.

He managed to hold back long enough to see and feel her second powerful climax, to catch her ragged moan of pleasure in his mouth, and then his own body went over the edge, a searing wave of satisfaction stronger than anything he'd ever known engulfing him, and he cried out hoarsely as he shuddered in the overwhelming force of his release.

"Now I know what you meant."

Her soft voice roused him, and Jared eased up onto his elbows. Her face was flushed and softened with a sensual exhaustion, her eyes dreamy. He kissed her because he had to and, realizing what she was talking about, murmured, "If I'd had the sense to be patient all those years ago, you would have known then."

A bit shyly she asked, "Did you feel—that—even then?"

He hesitated, then shook his head. "No, I never felt anything like what just happened between us. I suspected there was fire in you, but I didn't know if I could touch it."

Her breath flooded out in a shaky sigh. "I felt . . . out of control . . . and I *liked* it."

Jared smiled down at her. "If you have any question, so did I. And you weren't the only one out of control. You may have noticed we didn't make it to the bed."

She felt a different kind of heat rise in her cheeks as she glanced around at the big, lamplit living room. Thank God she'd closed the drapes; even thirty floors up they could have been observed from one of the nearby buildings.

Clearing her throat, she murmured, "No, we didn't, did we?"

"After all these days of patience," he said, his voice thickening slightly, "I'm surprised I had any control at all. God, Dani, I needed you so badly. . . ."

Her arms tightened around his neck and she lifted her head far enough to feather her lips along his jaw. Huskily she murmured, "Would you have let me leave San Francisco?"

"Yes. But I would have followed you." He found her mouth almost blindly, kissing her deeply. Followed her? He probably would have been no more than half a step behind her, turning his back on all his responsibilities here simply because he wouldn't have been worth the bullet to shoot him without her.

Walking away from her ten years ago had torn the heart out of him, but walking away now—or letting her walk away—would cost him his soul.

She was smiling up at him, the earlier weariness fading as her eyes grew sleepy with desire, and since he was still inside her, he knew she could feel the swelling renewal of his passion. She tightened around him and he caught his breath, sharp pleasure exploding in him.

"Do you think we'll make it to the bed this time?" she murmured, tightening her inner muscles again.

They didn't, but Danica didn't seem to mind. In fact, she protested sleepily when he eased away from her sometime later. But Jared had decided that his hunger for her had been momentarily satisfied, at least long enough for them to make it to the bed. He began to change his mind when he looked down at her body, languid gold against the pale carpet, but managed to control himself long enough to lift her into his arms and carry her from the room.

"I'm impressed," she said solemnly, halfway to the bedroom.

"Oh? Why?"

"Well, it looks so easy in the movies, but it has to take muscle to lift someone who weighs half your own weight up from the floor—and I probably weigh more than half."

"No, you don't," he replied, holding her slender body easily. "I weigh over two hundred, and you can't possibly weigh more than half of that. You're too delicate."

"I'm still impressed."

He chuckled. "My ego thanks you."

Instead of carrying her directly into the bedroom, where a lamp burned on the nightstand, he turned into the roomy bathroom just off it and flipped the light switch.

"Are we taking a shower?" she asked politely.

Jared grinned at her as he opened the frosted glass door of the big shower stall and set her on her feet inside, then joined her and pulled the door closed. "I thought we would."

"Don't I get a vote?"

"Of course you get a vote. All in favor of feeling my soapy hands touch every part of your body, say aye."

"Aye," she said a bit weakly.

The bathroom steamed up rather quickly after that, and it had little to do with the hot water. A soapy exploration was what Jared had in mind, and he was a thorough man.

Smoothing the lather over her delicate collarbone and down to her breasts, he said huskily, "Did I happen to mention how nicely you've filled out in the last ten years?"

Burning the instant he had touched her, Danica was gripping his shoulders to help keep herself upright. His hands were moving over her, warm and slippery, lifting and kneading the weight of her breasts, and she could barely think.

"I—I was just a teenager then," she managed unevenly, and gasped when his thumbs brushed her tingling nipples.

He bent his head and licked at the droplets of water clinging to her bottom lip. "You're all grown up now," he told her, sliding one soapy hand down over her stomach.

She couldn't believe he had aroused her yet again so soon after satisfying her completely, but when his fingers probed gently between her thighs, it ignited an explosion of heat deep inside her that spread outward like wildfire. She didn't know how she was able to remain upright, not with his hands exploring her body with the completeness he had promised, but somehow she was able to. She even found the strength to make a soapy investigation of her own, her hands gliding over his hard-muscled body, her breath catching at the sheer power of him.

Both of them were shaking by the time Jared turned the water off and pulled her from the stall. He wrapped a towel around himself and then dried her far more carefully, until finally she pushed the towel away, then wreathed her arms around his neck and lifted her face for his kiss.

The bed might have gotten a bit damp, but neither one of them really cared.

Jared stirred as Danica eased from his side, and felt yet another rush of desire drive off exhaustion as he watched her golden body gleam in the lamplight.

"Where are you going?" he murmured.

She opened her closet door and pulled out a silky robe, shrugging into it and tying the belt before she answered him, completely unselfconscious. "To the kitchen. I don't know about you, but I'm starving; it's after midnight."

He had to admit to a pang of hunger himself, which wasn't all that surprising considering the activities of the past hours. Sitting up, he said, "I could use a snack."

"You stay put; I'll bring us something in here."

Grinning at her, he said, "I could get used to that kind of service."

"Don't," she warned, but with a smile. Leaving him chuckling, she headed for the kitchen. She paused briefly in the living room, shaking her head somewhat bemusedly as she surveyed the wild scatter of their clothing. Her bra was dangling half off the coffee table, and her shoes seemed to have landed at opposite ends of the room. For heaven's sake!

She picked up the clothing, folding his neatly over the back of the chair and piling hers on the cushion. The torn panties made her shake her head again, feeling heat in her cheeks. He had been rather intense about wanting her, but then, she hadn't exactly been passive. Though she hadn't looked, she had the uneasy suspicion that she would find a few scratches on his back.

Still feeling dimly astonished at herself, she went on into the kitchen and began to raid the refrigerator.

In the bedroom, Jared had relaxed for a few moments before a sudden realization brought him upright in the bed.

After midnight.

It was actually closer to one A.M. he found when he checked his watch and looked at the alarm clock on Danica's nightstand. He swore softly and reached for the phone beside the clock. His first call was to one of his own phones at the hotel, which was connected to an answering machine. There were no messages.

He called a second number and waited through numerous rings before finally cradling the receiver. No reason to worry, he told himself as he settled back onto the pillows. No reason at all. He was easy enough to find here; certainly Max wouldn't have to think long before trying Dani's number.

She came back into the room a few minutes later, carrying a loaded tray, and the instant he looked at her everything else faded from his mind. Her thick dark hair had dried in its usual style, falling straight and shining to her shoulders, framing a face holding the delicate color some people called an afterglow— and which Jared found absolutely enthralling.

The fire in her nature wasn't hidden now; it showed in the liquid darkness of her eyes, in the sensuous way she moved, in the peculiarly feminine smile gently curving her lips. She was a woman of passion. His woman.

"God, you're lovely," he said huskily.

A bit startled but pleased, she said, "Men always say that to women carrying trays."

He took the tray from her so that she could join him in bed, placing it within reach of them both. "I would have said it even if you'd been empty-handed," he promised.

"We'll see soon enough," she murmured.

She had prepared enough food to satisfy a small army; the two of them polished off most of it easily. In the peaceful, lamplit quiet of the bedroom they talked, not about anything important; both of them had chosen to accept this night without question, to wait until morning to consider what came next.

For now it was enough that they were together.

When the food was gone and the tray returned to the kitchen, Jared found himself filled with a now familiar hunger, and he wasted no time in opening the silky lapels of her robe to find the silky flesh underneath.

"I can't seem to get enough of you," he told her, watching intently as his warm breath caused a nipple to tighten in anticipation.

"Good," she murmured, her body already burning and throbbing for his touch, his possession. Again. She didn't know where either of them was getting the energy and she didn't much care; with his hands and mouth on her, nothing mattered to her except him. Nothing at all.

It was nearly three A.M. by the time he reached over her to turn out the lamp on the nightstand, and Danica cuddled close to his side in sleepy, sated contentment. She had never been so wonderfully drained and had every intention of sleeping until at least noon.

The phone rang two hours later.

Wrenched from the depths of sleep, she was barely aware of Jared stirring beside her while she turned in his loosened embrace and fumbled for the receiver. It was still dark, and she peered at the luminous numbers of the bedside clock with indignant astonishment as she finally got the receiver up to her ear.

"Hello?"

"Dani, I'm sorry to wake you." Max's voice was as quiet and calm as it always was. "But if Jared's there, I need to talk to him."

"Just a minute." She reached to turn on the lamp and blinked at the brightness for an instant, then worked herself up into a sitting position. Her eyes felt scratchy and hot, and her head seemed to be stuffed full of cotton.

Jared pushed himself up on an elbow, coming fully awake more quickly than she because his job made him more accustomed to predawn phone calls. "What the hell?" he muttered.

"It's for you." She handed him the receiver and absently drew the sheet up over her breasts. "It's Max."

He frowned, his eyes instantly sharp and oddly apprehensive; his voice was edgy when he spoke into the phone. "Max, what is it?"

Danica couldn't hear the reply, but she came completely awake with a chill when she saw the color drain from Jared's face.

"How bad?" he demanded harshly, and whatever the answer was, it didn't do anything except set his ashen face in stone. "Where? What the hell was— never mind. Yeah, I know the address. I can be there in half an hour. Right."

Pushing himself upright, Jared leaned across Danica to hang up the phone, then immediately tossed back the covers on his side and left the bed.

"Jared . . . ?"

"I have to go," he said, his voice still harsh. He didn't look at her as he strode from the room.

Danica remained there for a minute or two in shock, then quickly slid from the bed and pulled on her silk robe. She went into the living room, finding him almost dressed, tucking his shirt into his pants and reaching for his gun.

"Jared, please talk to me," she said unsteadily. "Tell me what's wrong."

He buckled the shoulder holster into place and picked up his jacket, looking at her only as he shrugged into it. "There's . . . a problem," he said, not so harsh this time. "Something I have to deal with."

"But what—"

"Don't ask me any questions, Dani, please. I've already told you more than I should, and—" He sighed explosively. "God, this whole thing's insane!"

Frightened, she crossed the space between them, her hands lifting to his chest because she had to touch him. He instantly pulled her closer, both his arms wrapped around her with a force just short of pain.

Into her hair he muttered, "I'm sorry, baby, but I've got to go. I'll be back as soon as I can, all right?"

"Be careful," she whispered when he lifted his head.

His lips curved in a strained smile. "Don't worry, it isn't a dangerous problem. Not for me, at least, not this time." He kissed her briefly, then released her. "I'll be hours at least; why don't you go back to bed and try to sleep."

Danica nodded, but when the door had closed behind him and she was alone in the apartment, sleep was the furthest thing from her mind. And even though her mind was working on only two hours' rest after a somewhat exhausting night, what she had seen in Jared's white face had left her with a clear, cold head.

The trap, of course. Something had gone wrong with the trap, something bad enough to have shaken Jared deeply. But what?

The collection was still here, locked safely in the apartment's secret room, so that wasn't it. The museum? No, because he'd said that he knew the address, and Max wouldn't have questioned him on that point if it had been the museum.

What, then? *What?*

After a moment, Danica went to put the coffee on and take a shower. It would be light soon. She could open the drapes and look out on the city. Watch television. Maybe even work. But she wouldn't sleep.

Not until he came back to her.

SIX

Morgan was beginning to get tense about the entire situation. The collection would be moved to the museum within days, which meant the bait would be in the trap. Neither Max nor anyone else had deigned to inform her that there *was* a trap and she hadn't seen a sign of Quinn in more than two weeks.

It was maddening.

She didn't fool herself into believing that Quinn wasn't uppermost in her mind. Once she'd gotten over her fury at having been presented with a concubine ring—though she fully intended to give him a piece of her mind about *that* little item when next they met—she had gone back to spending an hour or two of her evenings parked outside some likely museum or jewelry store hoping to get lucky, as she had once before. Even after the mess she'd landed herself in the last time, and even knowing how reckless and dumb it was, she kept up the nightly search.

But the most elusive thief in the world seemed to have no difficulty in eluding her.

She had read the newspapers front to back and had kept her ears open during her days at the museum, and if Quinn had robbed anybody, they apparently didn't know it. There were no splashy headlines about the world-famous cat burglar, no breathless news bulletins on television, and nobody had reported a jewel or art robbery of any kind since Max, Wolfe, and Jared had captured a psychotic thief bent on murdering Storm.

In fact, barring a definite undercurrent of tension between Wolfe and Jared, things had been downright *peaceful*.

Morgan told herself she should be happy about that state of affairs. It was best for all concerned. Quinn had quite probably gone back to Europe, especially after she'd warned him about the trap.

Something she hadn't mentioned to Max.

Still, in spite of common sense and logic, she had the feeling Quinn hadn't left San Francisco. He was here somewhere, and if he hadn't committed a robbery, it was probably because he was waiting for a chance to grab Max's collection—trap or no trap. That was why she kept looking for him, she told herself. Because if the first warning hadn't worked, maybe she could come up with one he would pay attention to. It was, after all, her responsibility to guard the forthcoming exhibit from harm, and Quinn undoubtedly posed a threat she should guard against.

Yeah, right! She sneered at herself.

The simple truth was that she couldn't get him out of her mind. She had told Dani that she lived to see him in the daylight, and in a way it was true. She had seen him only at night, surrounded by the darkness he used to such good account, and though she had seen his unmasked face only briefly and in poor light, it was branded in her mind as clearly as if she carried a photograph of him.

She could have provided the police with a very accurate description of him. Did he know that? Of course he did. Did he worry about it? No, because he knew all too well she wouldn't say a word about him to the police.

Dammit.

She refused to wear the concubine ring, no matter how beautiful it was, but she hadn't exactly dumped it in the garbage either. In fact, she had a habit of taking it from her jewelry box and staring at it for long minutes each night before she went to bed. And wouldn't Freud have a field day with *that*.

On this particular Thursday night, Morgan had, with difficulty, talked herself out of her usual search for Quinn. She had occupied herself with paperwork and a late movie, then showered and dressed for bed in her usual comfortable sleepshirt. She paid a brief visit to her jewelry box and studied the glowing, square stone of the concubine ring, said a few heartfelt words about Quinn's probable ancestry out loud, and her feelings vented somewhat, went to bed.

When she woke with a start, the luminous display of her alarm clock proclaimed that it was twenty minutes after two in the morning. It was very quiet, but she found herself lying rigidly beneath the covers, wide-awake, her ears straining. Something had awakened her, she knew that. Something—

There. A faint sound from the front of the apartment, from the living room. A scratching sound, then a very soft creak, the way a floorboard protested weight.

Morgan held very strong views about guns. She believed that the vast majority of the people who owned guns probably couldn't be trusted with a slingshot, and she believed that anyone who had both a gun and a child of any age in the same house was guilty of criminal stupidity.

But Morgan had been on her own for too long to take dumb chances. So she had learned to handle guns from experts and had bought an automatic to keep in her apartment. Twice a month she went to a target range and practiced scrupulously to keep her aim true. She was, in fact, a crack shot.

So it was almost a reflex to slide very carefully from the bed, ease open the drawer of her nightstand, and take out the gun. It was another reflex to thumb off the safety and hold the weapon in a practiced two-handed grip.

Of course, it probably would have been smarter to creep into the bathroom with the gun and her portable phone—also on the nightstand beside her bed—lock the door, and call the police. But she didn't even think of that until much later. Instead she crept toward the door of her bedroom, ears straining, trying to be utterly silent.

The hallway was short, and she lingered close to the wall just outside the living room, searching the dark room for any sign of movement. There . . . by the window. It was only a shadow, indistinct, but it didn't belong there.

Remaining close to the wall for cover, her eyes fixed on the shadow, she warned in a grim voice, "I have a gun. And I'll use it, believe me."

"I believe you." The voice was deep, masculine, and somewhat dry. "However . . . since American authorities haven't yet put a price on my head . . . I'd rather you didn't. Shooting me for profit . . . makes perfect sense to me . . . but I'm not quite ready for a mercy killing."

She slumped. "Quinn."

"Don't sound . . . so damned relieved, Morgana," he reproved in an even drier voice. "I may not be a murderous fiend, but you should . . . at the very least . . . consider me a mild risk. I am a known felon, after all."

"You're a lunatic." Automatically she pointed the pistol at the floor as she eased the hammer back down and thumbed on the safety. She stepped into the living room and put the gun on a table by the wall, then turned on the lamp there.

It took a moment for her eyes to adjust to the sudden light, but when they did, she found him near the window, his gloved hands resting on the back of her high-backed reading chair. More disappointed than she wanted to admit to herself, she noted that his usual all-black cat-burglar costume included the ski mask that hid his face. Why was he hiding his face from her when she'd already seen it?

"What are you doing here, anyway?" she demanded.

"Happened to be . . . in the neighborhood," he murmured.

Morgan took a step toward him, then another, frowning. He was standing too still, she thought, too stiffly. And something about the way he was speaking wasn't right. "Oh, really? And you just *happened* to climb up my fire escape and pick the lock on the window?"

"Lousy lock," he said, his voice growing softer, almost slurring. "You . . . ought to get another."

Forever afterward, Morgan was never certain at what moment she knew what had happened. But she began moving toward him more quickly, covering the space between them with hasty steps. Maybe it was pure instinct that told her what was wrong—the primal sensing of blood and weakness—but she knew with utter certainty that he was very badly hurt. As soon as she was closer to him, the fact was obvious.

"No police, Morgana," he muttered in that soft, thickened voice. "Doctors have to report—report—" He swayed, and she was barely able to reach him in time to keep his head from striking the floor when he fell.

"Quinn? *Quinn?*" The black of his sweater showed a dull wet gleam high on his chest and on his left shoulder. A spreading gleam. And when she pulled the ski mask off, his lean, handsome face was ghostly pale and beaded with sweat, his flesh chilled. His eyes were closed.

Morgan had never felt so cold with fear, but first-aid training took over as she felt for the carotid pulse in his neck. His heart was beating, but faintly, and the rhythm was all wrong; he was going into shock.

He was far too heavy for her to move. Keep him warm and elevate his legs, she told herself with a calm inner voice that came from God knew where. She dragged a heavy blanket from her bed and covered him, then lifted his legs carefully until they rested across a low hassock. She didn't want to look at the wound, but knew she had to, and Quinn's last mumbled words kept ringing in her ears hauntingly. She couldn't call a doctor, because doctors had to report violent wounds to the police—and the police wanted Quinn in the worst way.

Even so, Morgan knew with absolute certainty that Quinn alive and in jail would forever be her choice over Quinn dead and still an enigma to the police; if she had to make that decision, it was already made.

She used her sewing scissors and carefully cut his sweater to expose the wound. She didn't know much about this kind of thing, but she was certain she was looking at a bullet wound. One glance was enough; she made a thick pad of several clean cloths and pressed it gently over the sluggishly bleeding wound, fighting a queasy feeling. But that cool inner voice remained calm inside her head.

Not so bad. The bleeding's nearly stopped. Unless there's an exit wound. . . . She slipped a hand under his shoulder and didn't know if she should be relieved that the bullet was still lodged in his body. *It isn't near the heart or lung. I think.*

"Damn you," she muttered, hardly aware of speaking aloud. "Don't you die on me, Quinn. Damn you, don't die."

Those absurdly long lashes of his lifted, and even now a gleam of amusement lurked in the darkened green eyes. "If you're going to swear at me," he said in a voice little more than a whisper, "then . . . at least use my first name."

"I don't know it," she snapped, holding on to her ferocity because she suspected it was the only thing that kept her from falling apart.

"Alex," he murmured.

She knew very well he wasn't lying to her. Alex was his name, his real name, and that knowledge put her several jumps ahead of just about everybody who was chasing Quinn. But she didn't feel any elation because he'd trusted her with the information. She was very much afraid that it might well be along the lines of a deathbed confession. Her voice held steady and grim.

"You die on me, *Alex*, and I'll hunt your ghost to the ends of the earth."

His eyes closed, but a faint chuckle escaped him. "I can save you . . . the search. You're quite likely to find me . . . in the neighborhood of perdition's flame, Morgana."

She tasted blood and realized she'd bitten her bottom lip. "I have to get a doctor for you—"

"No. The police. I can't let them put me away . . . not now. I'm too close."

She didn't know what he was talking about. "You have a bullet in you, and it has to come out." When his eyes opened again, she was even more alarmed by the feverish glitter stirring there. Quickly she said, "Max. I'll call Max. He'll be able to get a doctor here quietly, without the police having to know."

It didn't strike her until much later how wonderfully ironic her solution was: a wounded cat burglar bleeding in her living room, and the only man who might be able to help him was the man who owned a priceless collection that would soon bait a trap designed to catch that cat burglar.

Ironic? It was insane.

Quinn looked at her for a long minute, and then a sigh escaped him. Relief, acceptance, regret, or something else—she wasn't sure what it was. But the smile that briefly curved his lips was a strange one, twisted with something other than pain.

"All right. Call him."

Despite the fact that it was the middle of the night, Max answered his private phone line in a clear, calm voice and listened to Morgan's hasty explanation without interruption. When she was through, he simply said, "I'm on my way," and she found herself listening to a dial tone.

Quinn seemed to be unconscious, but he was still breathing. She tucked the blanket more securely around him and went back to her bedroom to quickly strip off her sleepshirt and scramble into jeans and a sweater. Then she returned to kneel beside him. Her fingers trembled as she stroked his thick golden hair and then his cool, damp cheek.

"If you die, I'll never forgive you," she whispered. He might have heard her, or he might have been too deeply unconscious to hear anything, but his head moved just a bit as if he wanted to press himself more firmly to her touch.

It was ten interminable minutes before she heard a quick, soft knock at her door and went to let Max in. She had turned on more lamps, so he was able to see Quinn clearly the moment he stepped into her apartment.

"The doctor should be here any minute," Max told her, shrugging off his jacket and tossing it over the couch before moving quickly toward Quinn. "How is he?"

"The same." She followed and knelt on one side of the unconscious man while Max knelt on the other. His long, powerful fingers checked the pulse, and then he eased the blanket back and looked under the cloths with which she had covered the wound. His hard face rarely showed emotion of any kind no matter what he may have been feeling, and his voice remained dispassionate.

"Nasty. But not fatal, I think."

If a doctor had said the same thing, Morgan probably would have doubted him, but she never doubted Max. The cold tightness of fear eased inside her, and she felt herself slump a little. "He—he looks so pale."

"Loss of blood." Max replaced the cloths and drew the blanket back up to Quinn's throat with a curiously gentle touch. "And shock. The human body tends to resent a bullet."

"It's still in him."

"I know." Max looked at her for a moment, then said, "I think he'd be more comfortable off the floor."

"If we can get him to my bed—"

"You go get the bed ready. I'll bring him."

Quinn was by no means a small man, but Max was unusually large and unusually powerful, and he seemed to feel little strain as he carried the unconscious thief into Morgan's bedroom and eased him down on the bed. Morgan helped pull his soft-soled boots off, then eyed the remainder of his lean, black-clad form hesitantly.

"Maybe I'd better do the rest," Max said.

She nodded and backed toward the door. "Maybe you'd better. I'll—go make some coffee."

She had just filled her coffee maker and turned it on when the doctor arrived. He was a middle-aged man, with steady eyes and a soft voice, and seemed quite matter-of-fact about having been pulled from his bed to treat a gunshot wound secretly. If Max said it was the right thing to do, he told her comfortably, then that was all he needed to know.

Morgan pointed the way to the bedroom, but retreated to the kitchen herself. She didn't know how much more she could take, but was fairly sure her fortitude would crumble if she had to watch a bullet being extracted from Quinn.

She could hear the low voices of the doctor and Max, and once a faint groan caused her to bite down hard on a knuckle. She turned the television on to an all-night news channel, but remained in the kitchen and was working on her second cup of coffee by the time Max came out of the bedroom a few minutes later.

"The bullet's out," he reported quietly.

Morgan poured him a cup of coffee and gestured toward the cream and sugar on the counter, then said rather jerkily, "I heard him. Did he . . . ?"

"He came to in the middle of it," Max explained. "It wasn't very pleasant for him, I'm afraid. But he doesn't want anything for pain, and he's still conscious."

"He'll be all right?"

"Looks like it." Max sipped his coffee, then added with a hint of dryness, "So you'll have a wounded cat burglar in your bed for a few days."

It occurred to Morgan that Max had been amazingly incurious about all this, and she felt heat rise in her face. Clearing her throat, she murmured, "I, uh, sort of ran into him again a couple of weeks ago, and he— more or less—saved my life."

"Did he?"

She nodded. "So I owe him. Giving up my bed for a few days isn't much of a price to pay."

Max was watching her steadily. "No, if he saved your life, I'd say it was a bargain."

"You won't—" She cleared her throat again and said with difficulty, "That was the night I overheard something I probably shouldn't have at the museum, Max."

"I thought you might have." He smiled slightly. "I saw your name in the museum's security log when I signed out, Morgan. I had a hunch you'd overheard Jared and me talking, and had figured out what we were planning."

"Yeah, well . . . after Quinn saved my life, I—warned him. About *Mysteries Past* being bait for a trap."

"I see."

"I'm sorry, Max, but—"

"It's all right," he soothed, but before he could say more, the doctor emerged from the bedroom with positive news.

"Constitution of an ox," he said, gratefully accepting the coffee Morgan offered. "And a quick healer, unless I miss my guess. Probably be on his feet in a day or two." He looked at Max and added, "He wants to see you, and I doubt he'll rest until he does."

Max set his cup on the counter, gave Morgan a slight, reassuring smile, and left the kitchen as the doctor was beginning to give her brisk instructions on how to care for the patient during the coming days.

When he entered the lamplit bedroom, Max stood for a silent moment studying Quinn. His upper body was slightly raised on two pillows, the covers drawn just above his waist, so that much of his broad chest and the heavily bandaged shoulder was clearly visible. His eyes were closed, but they opened as Max looked at him, clear and alert despite the pain he was undoubtedly in.

Curiously he didn't look incongruous in Morgan's bed. She hadn't gone overboard with frills in decorating her bedroom since she wasn't a frilly woman, but it was quite definitely a feminine room; despite that, Quinn seemed to fit among the floral sheets and ruffled pillow shams without sacrificing any of his maleness. It was an interesting trait.

After a minute or so, Max reached behind him to push the door shut. Quinn watched silently as the big, dark man moved gracefully over to the window and stood looking out on the dimly lighted street below.

"I gather Morgan doesn't know," he said quietly.

"No, she doesn't," Quinn responded, his voice subtly different from the careless one Morgan was accustomed to hearing.

"What kind of game are you playing with her?" Max asked evenly, still without turning.

Quinn shifted restlessly on the bed, grimacing slightly as his wound throbbed a protest. "You must know it isn't a game." There was an inflection in his voice: defensive, maybe even defiant. "I don't have the time or the emotional energy for games."

"Then keep her out of it." Max's words sounded with an authority rarely challenged, and even more rarely defeated. But a quiet challenge came from the bed.

"I can't," Quinn said.

Max stiffened just a little. "In some ways, Morgan's fragile. And she always roots for the underdog. You could break her heart."

Quinn said even more quietly, "I think she might break mine."

"Stop it. Now, before . . . either of you has to pay too high a price."

"You think I haven't tried?" Quinn laughed, a low, harsh sound. "I have. But . . . even in the dark, she shines. Glows with an inner fire. Like some precious jewel catching just enough of the light." He cleared his throat and went on with a stony control that did nothing to diminish the meaning of what he was saying. "I've tried to stay away from her. You'll never know how hard I've tried. I don't even remember deciding to come here last night. I just . . . came. To her."

Max turned then, leaning against the window frame, and the defeat was in his voice. "It's a hell of a mess, Alex."

Quinn's long fingers tightened their grip on the covers drawn up to his waist, and his mouth twisted as he met that steady, curiously compassionate gaze. "I know," he said.

Morgan had begun to worry when Max still hadn't left the bedroom after more than half an hour. The

doctor had gone, leaving her with instructions, anti-
biotics and pills for pain, and a list of supplies she'd
need to care for the patient, and all she could do
was pace the living room and eye that closed bedroom door nervously every time she passed the hallway. She couldn't hear a thing; what was going *on* in
there?

It was nearly dawn, after five o'clock, when Max
finally came out. As usual, he didn't show whatever he
was feeling, but she thought he was a bit tired.

"How is he?" she asked somewhat warily.

"Ready to sleep, I think."

Morgan was nearly dying of curiosity, but before
she could ask why Quinn had wanted to see him, a
sharp knock at her door distracted her. "Who could
that be? The doctor coming back for something?"

"No, I don't think so." Max moved past her to
open the door, and Jared Chavalier strode in.

Morgan moved almost instinctively to put herself
between Jared and the door of her bedroom, but her
eyes went to Max, and it was to him her thin question
was directed.

"How could you . . . ?"

"It's all right, Morgan," he said quietly with a
reassuring smile. "Trust me."

Before she could respond, Jared's low, angry voice
drew her attention. He looked a bit pale—probably,
she thought, from anger, since his eyes blazed with
it.

"Has anything changed from what you told me on the phone?" he asked Max.

Bewildered, Morgan realized that Max must have called from her bedroom phone while he was closeted with Quinn.

"No," Max replied. "Serious, but not fatal. He'll be all right in a few days."

Jared laughed shortly. "I might have known. He has more lives than ten cats."

Still calm, Max said, "You'll want to talk to him. He got close this time. Too close. That's why he was shot."

Morgan stepped away from the hall and into the living room as she realized there was no threat to Quinn from the Interpol agent. "I don't understand," she said to Max, her bewilderment growing. "What's going on?"

"*Mysteries Past is* bait for a cat burglar, Morgan, but it isn't Quinn. He's working with Interpol to help catch another thief."

Slowly she began to smile. "How about that."

Jared looked at her and, harshly, said, "Don't get any fool romantic notions about nobility into your head. Quinn's helping us to keep his own ass out of jail—and that's it. If we hadn't caught up with him, he'd still be looting Europe."

Morgan met that angry glare for a long moment, her smile fading. Then, speaking pointedly to Max, she said, "I'll go and make some fresh coffee."

"Thank you," Max said. When she was out of the room, he looked at the other man. "Was that necessary?"

Jared shrugged, scowling. He kept his voice low, but the anger remained. "Don't tell me you *want* her to fall for a thief. Aside from the fact that he's about as stable as nitro and damned likely to end up in jail or hanged—not to mention shot by someone with a better aim—he's just perfect for her. Hell, Max, you know he'll drift right out of her life the minute this is finished, if not sooner."

"Maybe not," Max said quietly. "He was hurt bad last night. Bleeding, in shock. He didn't come to me for help, and he didn't come to you. He came here. To Morgan. He doesn't remember making that decision."

"Then," Jared said crudely, "all his brains are below his belt."

"I hope you know better than that."

After a moment, Jared's eyes fell. "All right, maybe I do," he said. "But I thought I knew him ten years ago, and I was sure as hell wrong about that."

Max sat down on the arm of a chair near Jared and looked at him steadily. "What makes you more angry—that he became a thief, or that he didn't confide in you about it?"

"Does it matter?"

"Of course it does. If you're angry at what he chose to do with his life, that's concern for him. If you're angry because he didn't tell you, that's your bruised ego."

"Ego, hell. I'm a cop, Max, an officer in an international police organization. So how do you think I felt to find out that my brother was the crafty thief who had topped our most-wanted list for the better part of ten years?"

Morgan came back into the room just in time to hear that, and was so startled she spoke without thinking. "Brother? You mean, you and Quinn are . . . ?"

He looked at her with those pale, angry eyes, and for the first time she saw an elusive resemblance between his handsome features and Quinn's. "Yes, we're brothers," he confirmed flatly. "Do us all a favor and forget you know that."

She didn't get angry at him in return, because she was both perceptive enough to see the anxiety underneath his simmering fury and shrewd enough to have a fair idea of what a difficult position Jared must have found himself in when the infamous Quinn turned out to be his own flesh and blood. There was, clearly, reason enough for him to be a trifle put out.

"Consider it forgotten," she murmured.

Jared didn't look as if he believed her, but directed his question to Max. "Is he awake?"

"He was a few minutes ago."

"Then I'd better talk to him."

"Max, you said he was ready to sleep! Can't it wait until later?" Morgan protested.

"No," Jared told her briefly, and headed for the bedroom with a determined stride.

Morgan stared after him for a moment, then looked at Max. "Don't you think you'd better go in there too? Jared has blood in his eye, and Quinn's lost too much of his own to be able to defend himself."

"You're probably right." Max was frowning slightly, but he didn't waste any time in following Jared.

It was after eight o'clock that morning before Morgan found herself alone in the apartment with Quinn. Max and Jared had left together, both of them preoccupied, and Max had told Morgan that he would have the supplies she needed, as well as clothing for Quinn, delivered later in the day, and that he'd let everyone concerned know she wouldn't be coming in to the museum for a few days.

"Wolfe'll have a fit when he finds out what happened," Jared muttered gloomily, his anger apparently gone, but his mood not much improved.

"I'll handle Wolfe," Max told him.

"Good. He's still mad at me."

"Why should he have a fit?" Morgan asked curiously. "Good Lord, does *he* know Quinn too?"

"Ask Quinn," Jared growled, and stalked from her apartment.

Morgan, feeling her virtually sleepless and very eventful night by then, a state not helped by numerous cups of coffee, nearly wailed at Max, "And all this time I felt guilty because *I* knew him!"

One of his rare smiles swept across Max's hard face. "Morgan, since Alex is asleep, why don't you stretch out on your couch and take a nap. I think you need one."

That suggestion held too much appeal for her to argue, and it wasn't until she'd closed the door behind Max, briefly checked on her sleeping patient, and curled up on the couch with a pillow and blanket that something occurred to her.

Max had referred to Quinn by name only once, and then it had been his real name—Alex. She tried to think about that, but she was just too tired, falling asleep almost instantly.

"The doctor said you have to take the pills. They'll help prevent infection."

"Not with milk," Quinn said firmly, frowning up at her. "I hate milk, Morgana."

She sighed, faced with the first real mutiny from her patient after slightly more than twenty-four hours of tranquillity. He had slept most of that time, waking only briefly every few hours and accepting without protest the broth she had spooned into him. He had watched her steadily, his green eyes quiet, thanked her gravely for any service she performed for him, and was otherwise a model patient. Until now, anyway.

Given his personality as she knew it, she hadn't expected the placidity to last, of course, but she had hoped for at least a couple of days before he began to get restless.

"All right, no milk," she said agreeably. "But you have to take the pills. How about juice?"

"How about coffee?"

"The last thing you need is caffeine."

"Coffee," he repeated, softly but stubbornly.

Morgan debated silently, then decided it wasn't worth a fight. It was more important that he take the pills—no matter what he washed them down with. Besides, she was almost sure she had a jar of decaffeinated. "All right, coffee. It'll be a few minutes, though; I have to make some."

He nodded, those absurdly long lashes veiling his eyes, so she couldn't tell if he was gloating over her capitulation. She retreated from the bedroom with the unwanted milk, vaguely suspicious although she didn't know why.

Ten minutes later she returned to the bedroom to find the covers thrown back and the bed empty, and realized she must have read his intentions subconsciously if not consciously. His minor rebellion was escalating. The bathroom door was closed, and there was water running in the sink.

She set the cup of coffee on the nightstand, went to the door, and knocked politely. "Alex, what are you doing in there?"

"It's not polite to ask that, Morgana," he reproved in a muffled but amused voice.

She leaned her forehead against the door and sighed. "You're not supposed to be out of bed. The doctor said—"

"I know what the doctor said, but I'll be damned if I ever let myself get *that* helpless. There are some things a man prefers to do for himself. Do you have a razor?"

"You aren't going to shave!"

"Oh, yes, I am."

Morgan took a step back and glared at the door. "All right. I'll just wait out here until you get dizzy and fall on your—ego. When I hear the thud, I'll call Max and ask him to come over here and drag your carcass back to bed."

There was a moment of silence, and then the water stopped running in the sink and the door opened. He stood there a bit unsteadily, a towel wrapped around his lean waist, his green eyes very bright, and that crooked, beguiling smile curving his lips. He had slid his left arm from the sling meant to ease the weight on that shoulder and braced his good shoulder against the doorjamb.

Judging by the dampness of his tousled hair, he had washed up a bit, doing his best when he could hardly stand and wasn't supposed to get his bandaged shoulder wet. As for the towel—he probably hadn't felt steady enough to get into any of the clothing

Max had sent over, even though the stuff was neatly folded in plain view on the storage chest at the foot of Morgan's bed.

When Max had stripped him, he had removed everything; Morgan knew that because she had washed the pants and shorts and thrown the ruined sweater in the trash—not because she had given in to curiosity and looked beneath the covers for herself.

"You're a hard woman, Morgana," he murmured.

She wished she were. She had been trying rather fiercely to see him only as a wounded body needing her help, and as long as he'd remained in the bed, she had more or less succeeded. But he was on his feet now—however unsteadily—and it was impossible for her to look at him, wearing only a towel and a bandage, and not see him as utterly male and heart-catchingly sexy.

She remembered too well how that hard body felt against hers, and how his beguiling mouth had seduced hers until she hadn't cared who or what he was. She remembered his murmured words, when he'd told her that he thought she was going to break his heart.

She also remembered the mocking gift of a concubine ring.

It was that last memory that steadied her. Calmly she said, "Look, if you really have to shave, there's an electric razor around here somewhere. I'll get it for you. But you have to go back to bed."

After an instant, he nodded slightly and took a step toward her. He would have fallen if she hadn't quickly slid an arm around his waist and put her shoulder under his good one.

"Dammit, you tried to do too much," she muttered as he leaned on her heavily.

"I think you're right." He sounded definitely weakened. "If you could help me to the bed . . . ?"

Halfway across the room, Morgan got the distinct feeling that he wasn't quite as frail as he seemed, but she didn't try to call his bluff. What else could she expect, after all? she asked herself somewhat wryly as she helped him those last few steps. His humorous, mischievous, and careless nature had been obvious from the first time she'd met him, and she doubted very much if he had a sincere bone in his body; he was perfectly capable of pretending weakness simply because he enjoyed leaning on her.

She batted his amazingly limp but wonderfully accurate hand away from her right breast and more or less dumped him on the bed.

Quinn grimaced as his shoulder was jolted, but he was also laughing softly. "All right, but you can't blame me for trying," he said guilelessly.

Hands on her hips, Morgan glared down at him. Damn the man, it was so *hard* to stay mad at him! "Next time you get out of that bed, you'd better make sure you can get back under your own steam. I meant what I said about calling Max."

Quinn eased himself farther up on the bed, then glanced down at the towel still wrapped around him. "I suppose you wouldn't want to help me—"

"No. Like you said, there are some things a man should do for himself. I'll go find the razor." He was laughing at her again when she left the room, but Morgan didn't yell at him. She didn't even turn around to look at him, because he would have seen her smiling completely against her will.

Even if he *was* on the side of the angels this time, she told herself, he was still a thief and a scoundrel. Charming, but still a scoundrel. She needed to remember that.

When she returned to the bedroom a few minutes later, he was propped up on the pillows, the covers drawn up to his waist, sipping the coffee she'd brought him. The towel was crumpled up on the floor by the bed.

She retrieved it and returned it to the bathroom. Silently. She unwound the cord from the electric razor, plugged it into an outlet by the nightstand, and set the razor within easy reach for him. Silently. Then she gave him his pills and waited until he swallowed them.

He eyed her somewhat warily, then said, "You aren't mad at me, are you, Morgana?"

It cost her, but outwardly she managed to remain unmoved by his wistfulness. "No, but you're walking a fine edge," she warned him mildly.

He was silent for a moment, then set his coffee cup on the nightstand and nodded gravely. For once, his green eyes were perfectly serious. "I know—I can't help pushing. And . . . I hate having to depend on anyone else. For anything."

Morgan could feel her resolve weakening. As dangerous to her composure as his playful, amusing mode was, this—apparent—painful honesty was devastating. She had the sudden conviction that unless she was very, very careful, Quinn would steal far more from her than she could afford to lose.

From somewhere, she summoned an award-winning portrayal of calm reason. "Why don't we make an agreement. I'll do my best not to threaten your independence in any way, and you shelve Don Juan for the duration. Okay?"

Smiling, he nodded. "Okay."

"Good. Now, I'm going to do something about lunch while you shave. And afterward, if you don't feel like resting, there are a host of alternatives beginning with reading or television and ending with a card game."

"You play cards?" His eyes gleamed at her. "Poker?"

"Any kind except strip," she said gently.

"Oh, shoot," he murmured, not Don Juan now but the mischievous boy who was nearly as seductive.

She shook her head at him and turned toward the door, but halted there when he spoke softly.

"Morgana? Thank you."

Again she found her resolve threatened, and again she managed to shore it up. "Oh, you can pay me back easily, Alex. Just return the necklace you stole from me."

He laughed at her as she left the room, completely unrepentant and utterly shameless.

By Sunday morning Quinn felt well enough to get dressed and move around Morgan's apartment under his own steam. Max had come by with the doctor to check on his progress on Saturday, but other than those visitors they were alone together. True to his word, Quinn shelved his Don Juan persona, and she wasn't very surprised to find him an excellent companion.

He was a lively and amusing conversationalist, which she had known, never seemed to lose his sense of humor, could talk intelligently on any number of subjects, had seen a respectable chunk of the world, and played a mean game of poker. He even helped her in the kitchen.

Morgan didn't bring up the subject of why he was in San Francisco, ask him exactly what he'd been doing to get himself shot, or castigate him for not telling her the truth about his involvement with the *Mysteries Past* trap. Quinn didn't mention any of that either. She thought both of them avoided the more dangerous subjects, and though she didn't know his reasons, she certainly knew hers.

Quite simply, she didn't want him to lie to her—and she was half afraid he would.

They were casual with each other, and aside from one heated argument when Quinn wanted to give up her bed and sleep on the couch instead—Morgan won—they got along fine. But there was a growing awareness between them, perhaps the inevitable result of spending so much time together or perhaps something much more complicated, and by Monday night Morgan was clinging to her resolve with both hands.

She was afraid she was on the verge of doing something stupid, and she had the unnerved feeling he knew it too.

After they'd eaten dinner and cleaned up the kitchen, Morgan left him watching an old movie on television while she went to take a shower. She had gone out of her way to be conservative in her clothes, wearing mostly oversized sweaters and shirts with jeans and, at night, a pair of Oriental-style black pajamas that covered her decently by anybody's standards.

That night, however, she had unaccountably forgotten that the pajamas were in the dryer on the other side of the apartment, which meant she had to find something else to wear. Her choices consisted of either one of the very brief sleepshirts in which she slept when not nursing a wounded cat burglar or else a rather clingy gold nightgown, floor-length, with a green-and-gold floral negligee. Morgan debated only a moment before choosing the nightgown.

When she returned to the living room, the television was turned down low, only one lamp burned, and Quinn was standing by the front window—where he'd come in several nights before—gazing out at a chilly, foggy San Francisco night. He was wearing jeans with a button-up white shirt, the collar open and cuffs turned back loosely on his tanned forearms. The bandage on his shoulder didn't show, and he didn't look as if he'd ever been wounded.

"Is something wrong?" she asked immediately, wondering if he heard or saw something out there.

"No, I was just thinking . . . it's a good night for skulking around out there." He turned, but went still the moment he saw her.

Morgan felt oddly breathless. "Oh. Is this the kind of night you like? For—skulking, I mean."

He didn't answer immediately, and when he did, his voice was a bit husky. "It's the kind of night I'm used to. The kind of night I've seen a lot of. When the line between black and white blurs in the darkness."

She went slowly toward him, halting no more than an arm's length away. His size always surprised her when she was this close to him; because there was something so lithe and graceful about the way he moved, she tended to forget the sheer physical power of broad shoulders and superbly conditioned muscles. She had to tilt her head back to look up at him.

"Is that all you find nights like this good for?" she asked him softly. She could feel the heat of his body, and her own felt feverish. "What about when you're inside, like this?"

He drew a short breath and let it out roughly. "Something blameless, I suppose. Read a good book, watch television. Play cards."

"Strip poker?"

"A game you wouldn't play," he reminded her.

"Maybe I've changed my mind."

Quinn reached up with one hand to brush a strand of her long black hair away from her face, his fingers lingering for just a moment to stroke her cheek. His eyes were heavy-lidded, his mouth sensuous, and she could feel a slight tremor in his long fingers as they touched her.

Then, abruptly, he turned away and crossed the room to the hallway leading to the bedroom. "Good night, Morgana," he said briskly over his shoulder. Seconds later the bedroom door closed softly.

There wasn't much a woman could do when she had been rejected except wrap her pride around herself and try to put the rebuff behind her, so that's what Morgan did. She even managed to drop off to sleep somewhere around dawn.

When she woke up Tuesday morning, Quinn was gone.

SEVEN

It was almost noon on that Friday when Danica heard a soft knock at the apartment door. She hurried to answer it, the relief almost overwhelming when she saw him. He had changed clothes, looking more casual than usual in dark slacks and a sweater, and he wasn't wearing his gun. He looked tired but otherwise fine, and the way his eyes brightened when he saw her almost made up for the interminable morning.

He stepped inside, pushed the door shut behind him, and immediately gathered her into his arms. "Lord, you feel good," he muttered into her hair.

"So do you." She smiled up at him when he lifted his head, and responded to his kiss with matching hunger.

When he could, Jared said, "I'll never enjoy being dragged away from you, but coming back certainly has its points."

"Can you tell me now why you were dragged away?" she asked as they went into the living room.

Jared could see that she had been working; he recognized the Black Royal diamond cradled in a nest of cotton on her worktable. He guided her to the couch, and when she sat down beside him, he shook his head slightly.

"I'm not sure I want to."

Danica wasn't offended, but she was curious. "For security reasons?"

He looked at her somewhat wryly. "No, not that. But remember when we talked earlier about all the complications surrounding the *Mysteries Past* exhibit?"

"Yes. You were amused by my reaction."

Jared sighed. "Well, let's just say that the situation is getting more complicated with every passing day. It might be easier on us both if we just don't talk about it. Or at least not in any detail."

She eyed him. "Tell me this much—do the things you don't want me to know just yet really matter?"

"To us? No, because I will tell you everything once our trap either does or doesn't work." He smiled at her. "I'm not going to lie to you, Dani, but there are a few things I'd rather not have to explain right now."

Being a normal woman, she was definitely curious, but since she was blessed with considerable patience, she was willing to wait for her answers. "I suppose I can accept that," she told him. "As long as I eventually get the truth."

"Oh, you will." He paused, then frowned. "I suppose I'd better tell you about Quinn, though. If I don't, Morgan probably will."

"What about him?"

Jared debated for a silent moment, then spoke rapidly. "The trap we're setting isn't to catch Quinn. Because of circumstances I'd rather not go into, he's actually helping us. Sort of a . . . set-a-thief-to-catch-a-thief kind of deal."

Danica stared at him. Less preoccupied by the charismatic Quinn than Morgan, since she'd never met him, she asked a logical question. "Then who's the trap for?"

"Well, unlike Quinn, this one hasn't caught the fancy of the press or public, so there's been almost no publicity about his activities and you probably haven't heard of him. At Interpol, his code name is Nightshade."

Briefly distracted by the name, she said, "Isn't that another name for some plants, like belladonna?"

Jared nodded. "Pure poison. And he—or she, I suppose—is definitely that. A far more violent and dangerous personality than Quinn ever was. There have been eight killings committed during Nightshade's robberies in the past six years."

"You're right, I haven't heard of him. Does he work in Europe, or—"

"All over, but mostly here in the States. Every law-enforcement agency in the world has tried to identify him, and nobody's even come up with a name. No living witnesses we've been able to find, no fingerprints or other identifying evidence conveniently left behind, and the computers can't even find a pattern in the robberies, except that he favors gems and always leaves us his calling card. A dead rose."

She shivered. "That's a morbid touch."

"No kidding. You should hear some of the theories advanced by police shrinks and FBI behavioral experts. The general consensus is that aside from his love of gems and his tendency to kill anyone who gets in his way, Nightshade probably has a few more kinks in his nature."

"It sounds like it. And this is the person you're trying to trap?" She tried not to let that frighten her, and if she wasn't successful, at least she managed to keep the fear inside.

"Well, examining his crime scenes after the fact sure as hell hasn't gotten us any closer to him. And given the number of gems in the world, it's been nothing short of impossible to predict where he'd show up next. And we've tried, believe me."

Danica thought about it. "So . . . you decided to dangle a bit of irresistible bait. It's likely that a collection as priceless as Max Bannister's going on public display for the first time in more than thirty years would lure Nightshade here to San Francisco. And if you know he's here, you can set a trap to catch him."

"That's the idea," Jared agreed.

"Won't he suspect a trap?"

"If he's as smart as I think he is, he will. But greed tends to undermine common sense." Jared shrugged. "It's the only shot we've got, Dani. In six years, he hasn't put a foot wrong, and the odds are against him making a serious enough mistake in the future to let us catch him. And even if he does, God knows how many people will have to die first. So . . . we're going to try luring him to a trap designed just for him."

Danica didn't have to be told that all this information was shared by very few; she was mildly surprised Jared had told her. Still, she couldn't help asking curiously, "What part does Quinn play in all this?"

"He's . . . our eyes on the dark side of the streets. He has contacts, informants we couldn't get near. And he can stick his nose into places without the benefit of a door key or a search warrant."

For the first time, Jared seemed faintly uncomfortable. It didn't really surprise her; he must have found it galling to work with a thief, even to catch another.

Since he'd said he didn't want to go into the "circumstances" that had led to Quinn tossing his hat into Interpol's ring, Danica didn't ask about that.

Instead she said, "And none of your superiors know about this plan? Or the San Francisco police—barring the commissioner and one lone inspector?"

"That's right. Just those of us directly involved with *Mysteries Past*. If the plan works, we'll all be praised to the skies."

"And if it doesn't?"

"I'd rather not think about that." Then he shrugged. "I could certainly lose my job. Wolfe could lose his. And Max could lose his collection. It's a hell of a gamble."

"And dangerous," she said quietly. She kept remembering the distraught expression on his face this morning when he had left her. And she kept remembering that Nightshade seemed to have a fondness for killing.

Jared looked at her broodingly for a moment, then sighed. As if he'd read her thoughts, he said, "When Max called this morning, it was to tell me that Quinn had been shot last night. Not mortally, but bad enough."

Danica frowned. "What was he doing to end up being shot? I mean, the collection isn't in place at the museum yet. The trap isn't set."

"No, but Quinn's convinced that Nightshade is already in the city. That he might even live here. So he's been . . . looking around."

"Breaking into private homes?"

Wincing slightly, Jared said, "I told him not to tell me about it if he did. He claims he's mostly kept an eye on the nightly activities in the city, just to identify the players more than anything else. But since we're convinced Nightshade is a collector, searching for a secret cache in a private home is probably not a bad idea."

"Was that what he was doing?"

"No, he says he was near the museum last night—our museum, where the collection will be—and spotted someone apparently casing the building. He intended to follow this person back to, presumably, a house, apartment, or hotel. Unfortunately somewhere near the waterfront, his quarry doubled back and caught him. Shot him with a silenced automatic."

After a moment's thought, Danica said, "Couldn't that bullet be used as evidence? I mean—"

"I know what you mean. Yeah, if we ever do get our hands on this guy, if he has a gun, and if a ballistics expert can match it to the bullet a doctor dug out of Quinn's shoulder, we could at least hang an attempted-murder charge on him. The bullet's on its way to an expert now. What I'm interested to see is whether that bullet matches the ones taken from four of Nightshade's previous victims."

Danica understood what he was getting at. "If it does, you'll know that Nightshade is in the city, and that Quinn came awfully close to him last night."

"Right." Jared eyed her for a moment, then smiled. "I thought we weren't going to talk about this."

"One last question?"

"I'll have to hear it."

"Where is Quinn now? I mean, surely he isn't in a hospital. Don't doctors have to report gunshot wounds?"

Jared cleared his throat. "They do, and no, Quinn isn't in a hospital. Max got a doctor, who actually makes house calls, to treat him secretly. He's at Morgan's apartment."

Danica turned completely toward Jared, put her elbow on the low back of the couch, and propped her chin on her hand. She looked extremely thoughtful. "Morgan's apartment?"

"Uh-huh. That's where Max called me from this morning. Instead of trying to get to me or Max—whose place was closer to where he was shot, by the way—Quinn went to Morgan."

"And he's there now?"

"Now, and for the next few days, I gather. Until he's back on his feet."

It was Danica's turn to clear her throat. "I see what you mean about the situation getting more complicated."

"You don't know the half of it," he muttered somewhat ruefully, remembering Wolfe's reaction.

Max had indeed been able to "handle" Wolfe, but the interlude in his office at the museum hadn't exactly been pleasant. Since Wolfe hadn't yet forgiven Jared for, among other things, risking Storm's life by not giving her information that would have made her more cautious, he was quick to blame Jared for the latest misadventure as well.

"And you don't want to tell me," Danica said.

He turned a bit more toward her so that they were facing each other. She was wearing a severely tailored man's-style shirt in a rich gold color over dark slacks, and she looked incredibly feminine and heart-catchingly lovely.

"I've already told you more than I meant to," he said, unable to resist the urge to reach out and touch her gleaming dark hair and warm cheek. "The rest can wait."

Danica nodded, willing to accept that. "All right, I won't ask you any more questions. For now. Except . . ."

"Except what?"

"Well, with Quinn temporarily out of commission and the collection safely here, doesn't that mean you're going to be at loose ends for a while?"

"I suppose so," he murmured.

She nodded gravely. "And I'm so close to finishing the work, it's just a matter of hours now. I can easily get it done by the middle of next week even if I take the next couple of days off. Do you think Max would mind if I did?"

"I don't think he'd mind a bit," Jared told her, and pulled her into his arms.

The weekend was a peaceful one, for them. They spent most of the time in the apartment, still really getting to know each other even now that they were lovers. Uninterrupted by badly timed phone calls or any other outside demands, they slept together, cooked and ate together, bathed together—the shower stall remained a favorite place, but the huge oval tub in the apartment's largest bathroom proved to have an appeal all its own—and became so attuned to one another that they sometimes seemed telepathic.

Sunday was such a beautiful day they decided to go out and enjoy it, winding up in the early afternoon relaxed on a sunny patch of grass in a secluded corner of a park.

Lying back with her eyes closed, Danica murmured, "Today, it actually feels a little bit like summer. Do you remember that summer in Paris? At first, I mean. In the beginning."

"Of course I remember." His shadow fell over her face as Jared raised himself on an elbow beside her and blocked the sunlight.

She opened her eyes and looked at him, feeling her heart begin to beat with a quickening rhythm. Just looking at him, seeing the intent, absorbed expression in his eyes as he gazed down at her, just that was enough to arouse her.

"I remember how sweet you were then," he murmured huskily. "Shy and half-afraid of me. I remember how the sunlight found hints of fire in your hair, the way it does now. I remember the fresh smell of a summer storm coming in our bedroom window at night while you lay in my arms. I remember waking up in that hot apartment, the covers kicked away from us, and watching you sleep all sprawled and boneless, so lovely it broke my heart just to look at you. . . ."

Danica wanted to ask him if he remembered the months that had followed, the escalating tensions, the arguments and hostile silences, and the growing distance between them, but she thought the bad memories were fading for him just as they were for her. It was almost impossible to remember all that with any emotion except faint surprise, because it seemed the bad things had happened to two other people, not them.

She reached up to touch his face, loving the way he felt under her fingertips. "Sometimes I saw you watching me . . . just the way you are now . . . and though I didn't really understand the look in your eyes, it made me feel so strange. I felt . . . hot and breathless and . . . naked."

Jared turned his head to press his lips to her palm, his eyes heavy-lidded. Then he leaned over her and very slowly began to unbutton her pale green blouse.

She caught her breath, and her hand slipped to the nape of his neck. "We can't . . . this is a public park."

"And we have this corner of it all to ourselves," he murmured huskily. When her blouse was unbuttoned to her waist, he opened it slowly and bent to trail his lips along the lacy cup of her bra. The front fastening gave way at his touch, and his mouth pushed the material aside.

Danica closed her eyes and bit back a whimper at the unbearable ache when he teased her tightening nipples with tiny flicks of his tongue. He was always able to awaken her desire swiftly, but out here with thick grass beneath her back and the sunlight warming her flesh, the hunger he ignited in her was instant and overpowering.

"Someone could find us here," she murmured, but even then she was coping with the buttons of his shirt, opening it up so that she could slide her fingers into the thick mat of hair on his chest and explore his hardness. "We could—we could be arrested."

"You forget. I'm a cop." He reached down and caught the hem of her skirt, drawing it up as he shaped her bare leg, until the light floral material was gathered at her waist.

Danica couldn't believe how incredibly sensual it felt to lie there on the sun-warmed grass, her clothing opened or pushed out of the way but not discarded. Nothing was discarded except her panties, and when he stripped them down her legs, she could only make a shaky sound of need and part her thighs for his touch.

God, she was so wanton, so completely and utterly abandoned when he touched her, that nothing mattered except feeling his hands on her, and his mouth, and aching because she had to have him inside her. She probably wouldn't have noticed if someone *had* strolled by because all she could see or hear or think or feel was him. . . .

Jared shrugged out of his shirt, but his pants and shorts were shoved down only as far as necessary, and when he entered her, sheathing himself in her pulsing heat, she cried out and tightened her legs to draw him in even deeper.

Neither of them was capable of prolonging the loving. They were both driven wildly toward release, their bodies mindless in need, caught up in the raw, primitive act of mating. On the sweet-smelling summer grass and underneath the boundless canopy of a clear blue summer sky, they gave themselves and took each other with a passion that was absolute.

When it was over, when their hearts had stopped pounding and their breathing had steadied, when the disarranged clothing was put back into place, they were both completely silent. They didn't break their physical contact even once all the way back to the apartment, holding hands or touching in some other way, and their glances met and clung often.

They didn't talk about what had happened, but it had changed them. Something had been bridged— past to present perhaps—and the tentative first stage of their relationship was over. It was almost as if they had been together for ten years, from the innocence and arrogance of youth to the knowledge and empathy of maturity.

They were no longer strangers.

Danica carefully repacked a stunning emerald necklace in its box and looked up from her worktable as Jared came out of the bedroom, where he'd been using the phone. It was shortly before ten o'clock on Tuesday morning.

"Any news?" she asked him.

"Umm. Max says Morgan's back at the museum this morning, and she isn't saying much."

"Quinn?"

"She said he was gone when she woke up."

Danica drew off the white cotton gloves she wore when working and shook her head a little. "From what Morgan's told me, he sounds like a very charming scoundrel at best. He came to her when he was hurt— but will he hurt her?"

"I honestly don't know." Jared picked up his jacket from the back of the couch and shrugged into it. He had gradually moved most of his belongings from the hotel to this apartment, and Danica had suggested the previous night that he complete the move since Max had offered them the use of the apartment as long as they remained in San Francisco.

That was as close as they had come to talking about the future.

"Will you see him tonight?" she asked. Jared had told her that until Quinn's injury, they had either talked or met every night to discuss progress.

"Yeah, if he calls in. I'll have to check the answering machine at the hotel until he does. I didn't think about giving him this number, and neither did Max."

Danica knew that Jared wanted to tell Quinn he *had* been shot by the same gun used on Nightshade's previous victims; that information had come from the ballistics expert late on Monday, and no one had gotten the opportunity to tell Quinn.

The virtually certain knowledge that Nightshade was indeed in San Francisco was going to make all concerned feel increasingly edgy, Danica knew; the collection was to be installed in the museum on Friday, a transfer now being meticulously planned by Jared, Max, and Wolfe, and after that their trap would be baited and set.

"I'll probably be gone until early afternoon," Jared told her now, and came to pull her into his arms. "I expect you to miss me terribly."

Responsive as always to his touch, she kissed him back and then smiled up at him. "I expect I will."

She did miss him when he was gone, but kept herself busy completing her work. He was with her for meals usually, and in the evenings—except when he went out twice in the following few days to meet with Quinn—so they still managed to spend quite a lot of time together.

On Friday, the Bannister collection was quietly moved from the apartment's safe room to the museum much as it had been moved once before, packed in mislabeled boxes and carried by innocent-looking moving men who were armed and experts in security.

The move went without a hitch.

Danica spent most of Friday in the museum, helping Morgan to unpack the collection, verify each item with its appraisal and the original inventory list, and arrange the pieces in their specially designed display cases. If the vibrant brunette was heartsick, she certainly didn't show it; in fact, she seemed quite cheerful and completely untroubled by despondent thoughts of charming cat burglars who came and went by night.

The exhibit's wing was heavily guarded by armed personnel while the collection was being readied for display, since the electronic security system could go completely on-line only after everything was in place. The only visitors were those directly concerned with *Mysteries Past*. Both Jared and Wolfe remained close by, alert and still a bit tense with each other, and Max was also in the museum all that day.

Danica had no idea where Quinn was and hadn't asked, but she thought he was probably near.

Though the collection was in place by closing time Friday, the wing would remain closed off for the next two weeks. There would be a private showing halfway through that period, during which the museum would be open only to invited guests, and then, a week later, *Mysteries Past* would open to the general public.

Nothing occurred to hinder any of the plans. The collection was installed safely, and the security system designed by Storm went on-line smoothly.

The weekend passed peacefully enough, and on Monday morning, as planned, the newspapers announced that the Bannister collection was in the San Francisco Museum of Historical Art and being readied for its presentation as the *Mysteries Past* exhibit.

"Do you hope to lure him before the exhibit opens?" Danica asked Jared curiously.

"Realistically? No. I think he'd be a fool to go after the collection so soon when it's going to be on exhibit for two months. But we have to be ready just in case."

They were talking early Tuesday morning. Danica was lying in bed watching him dress; Jared had to be at the museum before it opened for the day because Storm had suggested they do a daily test of every thread in their security net, just to make certain there were no weaknesses except the planned one.

Stretching languidly, Danica said, "Well, since you're going to be occupied all morning by your test and by that last security check of names on the list for the private showing this weekend, I think I'll go shopping. I hadn't planned to be here longer than a couple of weeks, and besides, I need something fancy for the private showing. Morgan says everybody'll be dressed to the teeth."

Jared bent over the bed, bracing his hands on either side of her, and kissed her. "You'd look beautiful in sackcloth," he murmured.

"I thought something sequined might be more apt," she told him gravely.

"You'll look good in that too," he agreed just as solemnly. And kissed her again.

When he'd gone, Danica remained in bed only a little while before getting up. She showered and dressed casually in slacks and a sweater; the day promised to be sunny but chilly according to the forecast provided by the morning news program she watched on television while she was brushing her hair. Since she and Jared had raided the kitchen in the middle of the previous night, she wasn't hungry for breakfast, and decided she could wait until their planned lunch later in the day.

There were numerous shops all around the apartment building, so she decided there was no need to call a taxi. She'd probably end up with aching legs from climbing the hills, she thought ruefully, but the fresh air would surely do her good.

It was just before nine o'clock when she went down to the lobby. She signed out as usual; the security precautions for the building remained in effect, though there was now only one guard in the lobby and a second one in another room monitoring the video cameras throughout the building.

"Going out alone, Miss Gray?" the guard asked, faintly surprised.

She smiled at him. "Yes, for once."

"Do you need a taxi?"

"No, I think I'll walk. With all the shops around here, I should be able to find what I need close by."

"Yes, if you can stand the hills."

Danica was still smiling when she left the building. The air was definitely chilly, but it was invigorating rather than cold, she thought, and the sunshine was pleasant.

"The coldest winter I ever spent," she murmured to herself, "was a summer in San Francisco." That old joke was proving to be the simple truth.

She flipped a mental coin and turned left in front of the apartment building. She'd seen enough while coming and going to know that there were stores all around, but she thought she remembered seeing a very elegant boutique in this direction with a number of stunning gowns in the window.

As it turned out, she never did get to that boutique.

"Hello, Danica."

Startled, she halted on the corner and looked at a man who, at first, was only vaguely familiar. Just slightly taller than she was, he was built powerfully with broad shoulders and very little neck. Not a handsome man, he had nothing especially memorable about him—except for the odd flatness of his blue eyes.

Danica remembered who he was then, but it was too late. The businesslike revolver in his hand made escape impossible.

The security guard could not pinpoint why he felt uneasy. He knew the Bannister collection was no longer in the building, and he hadn't noticed anyone suspicious in the area—but the hair on the back of his neck was standing straight up, and he'd been a guard too long to ignore that kind of danger signal.

He couldn't leave the building without being relieved at the desk, but he could go to the front door and lean outside so he could see both corners. He looked to the left first because he'd seen Miss Gray turn that way.

If he'd been even a minute later, he probably wouldn't have seen a thing. As it was, all he saw was a dark blue sedan pull away from the curb. The angle was all wrong for him to get even a glimpse of the license plate, but he did see something he knew instantly was wrong.

Miss Gray was driving.

He hesitated only a moment as the car disappeared, trying to fix what little he'd seen in his mind. The passenger had been a man, he was sure, and he'd been holding something that had looked a hell of a lot like a gun.

Under ordinary circumstances, the guard might have doubted his eyes enough to mentally explain away what he'd seen. But the security arrangements surrounding Miss Gray had been intense, and Jared Chavalier had the look of a man who would—and could—take this town apart if anything happened to his lady.

It didn't take long for the guard to find the number Chavalier had left in case of emergency, and within minutes he was tersely reporting what he'd seen.

EIGHT

She's gone.

Two words, each one syllable, short and agonizing. They kept echoing in Jared's mind, over and over, stabbing him like daggers. *She's gone.* He had thought the danger to her past, had thought her safe, or else he never would have—*She's gone.* Taken away from him so easily, just taken . . . Her smile this morning, so lovely, her hair spread out on the pillow like gleaming dark silk, her eyes glowing . . . *She's gone.*

"It doesn't make any sense," Wolfe said evenly, watching Jared rather carefully. "The collection's here in the museum, and that was reported all day yesterday in the newspapers and on television. Why would anyone grab Dani now?"

She's gone.

"You'd think one of us would be a more likely target," Storm agreed, also watching Jared. "We could be expected to know more about the museum's security than Dani; she was only here a couple of times."

She's gone.

Slowly Max said, "Whoever it is must have been watching her. For days at least, maybe longer. I can't believe he just happened to get lucky and stumble across her the first time she went out alone."

She's gone.

Morgan stuck her head into the slightly crowded office just then, and her quiet words were directed to Max. "It was Keane," she said, referring to the phone call that had drawn her across the hall to her own office. "He's back at his office. Nothing. He went up and down those streets for hours, and so did those detectives you sent over there. The only person who took any notice of what happened on that corner this morning was the guard; his description of the car is all we've got."

It was three o'clock that afternoon, and they were gathered in the largest office at the museum, the curator's office, since he was gone for the day and none of the other offices would begin to hold them all. Max and Dinah; Wolfe and Storm; Morgan and Jared.

Jared was half sitting on the big mahogany desk, unnaturally still. He wasn't looking at anyone, and he hadn't said a word for nearly an hour.

Wolfe, who was sitting behind the desk, shook his head at Morgan's news, and his voice roughened. "How the hell do we find one dark blue sedan in a city of this size?"

"We don't," Max said matter-of-factly. "So there has to be something else. Something we've overlooked."

Max was leaning slightly, his hands on the back of a chair where his lovely redheaded wife sat, and he looked down at her as Dinah turned and spoke to him quietly.

"Remember what happened with the thief who tried to use me?"

"I'm not likely to ever forget," he replied, his voice as calm as always but something dangerous flashed in the depths of his gray eyes.

She put one of her small hands over one of his much larger ones in a quick touch. "What I mean is— he threw all of us off for a while because we were so busy looking at the wrong thing. We thought he was after the collection."

"And he wasn't." Jared's voice had gone somewhere beyond strained, but he was looking at Dinah with eyes that saw her, and it was clear her words had reached into his anguish. "He wasn't after the collection."

They were all watching him again, and it was Wolfe who said, "If not the collection, then why—"

"Something else," Jared muttered, more to himself than to the others. "God, why can't I think? Something else . . . something personal . . . maybe a grudge, or—" He straightened suddenly, staring at Max. "What was it you said that first day? Something about the last job she had just weeks ago? That she wouldn't talk about it for security reasons, but you'd found out something about her spotting a fake?"

Max nodded slowly. "She was to authenticate a set of European crown jewels, according to my source. Somebody had tried to pull a switch, and she caught it."

"But was *he* caught?" Jared demanded intensely. "The one who tried to switch the stuff, was he caught?"

"I don't know."

Wolfe had reached for the phone on the desk and was already punching a number. "I'll bet somebody at Lloyd's knows," he muttered.

Max turned to look at Morgan, who was in the doorway. "And maybe my source knew more than he told. It was Nevin Sheridan, Morgan, could you try to get him for me, please?"

"From the British Museum? He'll be at home; it's after eleven P.M. over there."

Max rattled off a number, adding, "If you get him on the line, call me. He won't talk to you."

"Gotcha," she responded, and immediately disappeared back across the hall to her office.

Jared looked at his watch and swore softly. God, he felt so damned helpless! He couldn't get anyone on the phone from his Paris office at this hour, and there was no way for him to get information from there otherwise without a computer linkup. And the museum's computer system was self-contained, no modem to call outside—

As if she'd read his mind, Storm said quietly, "If Wolfe and Max can't get the details from their contacts, I can patch the computer here into the phone line in less than ten minutes so we can access Interpol's mainframe. But we need a name, Jared. A date, something."

"I know."

"Don't worry. We'll find her."

"Yes."

He had to find her. It was simply unbearable to consider any other alternative.

It had happened so fast that at first Danica wasn't really afraid. Bewildered, yes, but not afraid. Not until he directed her to drive south and they left behind the more congested areas of the city. Not until he had her park the car near a small, old house set back from the road and almost eerily isolated from any other houses.

That was when she began to be afraid.

He herded her into the house, still holding the gun in a businesslike manner. Without giving her time to do more than glance around at the worn furniture and uninteresting decorations of a rented-furnished property on a downhill slide, he urged her through the house. Pausing in the kitchen only long enough to light an oil lamp, he had her open the cellar door and descend the creaking stairs, carrying the lamp while he followed.

"Set it on the floor," he said when they'd reached the bottom of the stairs.

He was too far away for her to be able to use the lamp as a weapon, and he was between her and the stairs. She set the lamp on the floor.

"Back up. Until you reach the wall."

Danica obeyed, and by now the fear was twisting inside her, cold and sickening. "Why did you bring me here?" she asked as steadily as she could.

"Because this is the best place for my plans."

"Plans? What are you talking about?"

In the flickering glow of the oil lamp shining up from the floor, his face was set in a primitive cast, shadowed, demonic. His eyes gleamed with heat and hatred. His voice was soft, eerily gentle.

"After I saw you here, at the airport, and followed you to the apartment building, I spent a lot of time thinking about how I was going to make you pay. I had a lot of time, because he was guarding you so carefully. So, while I watched, I thought about it. I could have just killed you, of course, but that would have been too quick. Too easy."

"I didn't deliberately destroy you, and you know that," Danica managed to say quietly. "You must know it. It was my job to authenticate the jewels. I had no idea it was you who had tried to substitute paste copies."

He tilted his head slightly, as if listening to her, yet when he spoke, it was obvious he wasn't interested in her defense. "I kept remembering how you looked at me when I asked you out that first day," he murmured. "The surprise, as if you couldn't believe I would dare to think you could go out with me."

Danica half closed her eyes, stunned. He had misunderstood her surprise, seeing haughty rejection where there had only been her usual dismay at being the focus of male attention. She always retreated behind a wall of reserve at such moments and had never suspected her remoteness might be viewed as an insult.

"No," she said carefully, "that wasn't it, wasn't what I was thinking. It was just that I never get involved with anyone while I'm working—"

He laughed suddenly, harshly. "Oh, no? You got involved with somebody here quick enough. You couldn't wait to crawl into bed with him."

Desperate to lessen the rage she could feel building in him, she said, "You don't understand. Jared and I were married years ago, long before I met you. And I—I never really got involved with anyone else after he left me. Now we're trying to make it work again—"

He shrugged. "You'd say anything, you think I don't know that? All of you are natural liars. But I'm too strong to believe you. I've set my course, and nothing is going to change it." He smiled. "You have to pay for what you've done to me."

Danica would have backed away from the menace coming off him in waves if she could have, but she was cornered, the cold stone wall at her back. It took every ounce of control she could muster, but she managed to hold her voice steady. "What are you going to do?"

"I'm going to break you," he replied very gently. "Destroy that haughty disdain of yours. It's going to take a long time, I think, and I'll enjoy it very much. Step-by-step I'll strip away the layers protecting you until there's nothing left but the primitive need to survive."

Her skin crawling, nausea churning in the pit of her stomach, Danica shook her head helplessly. "No. Please—" She had to be calm. *Calm.* "Paul, you know this is wrong—"

"I wasn't sure how to go about it at first," he went on conversationally, "but I've been reading up on ways and means. The hostage mentality. Methods of torture. Psychological terrors we all have in common. Take the dark, for instance. Even people who think they aren't afraid of it really are. Given enough time spent completely alone and surrounded by total blackness. So that's first."

"Don't do this. Don't make the situation worse for yourself, Paul, please."

He ignored the plea, the appeal to consider his own future. It was as if he didn't hear her.

"It's a good thing I remembered this place. I used to play here as a child whenever we visited my aunt.

And it's just the way I remembered. This cellar is perfect for my needs. It's small, damp, warm enough, soundproof—and you're not going to believe how dark it will be as soon as I leave. You won't know how much time has passed, or what's going on in the outside world. And pretty soon you won't care. The only thing you'll be interested in, Danica, is pleasing me. You'll be desperate to please me, because I'll be the only one who can give you what you need to survive. Food. Water. Light."

"No," she whispered.

"Oh, yes. You'll do anything for me, Danica. Anything I ask. I'll enjoy that. First, I'll turn you into my own personal whore. I'll use you. Degrade and humiliate you. Teach you how to beg. And when I get tired of that, there are other ways to break the mind and destroy the flesh. Lots of other ways."

Danica didn't say a word as he picked up the oil lamp, and she managed not to cry out in protest when he carried the precious light to the stairs and up.

"Have a nice night, Danica," he said mockingly. "A nice, long night." Then the ponderous door thudded closed, the heavy, sturdy slide of a bolt rasped into place, and the light was gone.

The darkness was so absolute it had a texture, thick and heavy. For an eternal moment, Danica couldn't breathe, smothered by the awful weight of blackness. Then she slumped against the wall, a ragged intake of air at least proving that the sullen darkness grudgingly provided oxygen.

But that was all it provided. The cellar was completely bare; she had seen that clearly enough before he had taken the light away. There was nothing on which to sit or lie down except the hard cement floor.

She had the unnerving sensation of space around her coupled with the terror of not being able to *see* anything.

Her ragged breathing was the only sound, and it was loud. Too loud. She tried to silence that, to listen, hoping for some other sound. And after a moment or so, her straining ears caught something. Perhaps real, perhaps existing only in her tortured imagination. A skittering noise, faint, almost inaudible, yet holding the power to stop Danica's heart.

Oh, God, no . . .

Spiders.

"Paydirt," Wolfe said, already dialing another number as he spoke to Jared. "Only one person could have tried to switch copies for the jewels Dani was called in to authenticate, and he disappeared before they could get their hands on him. His name is Paul Galloway."

Storm was frowning. "If he got away, why try to get even with Dani?"

Max and Morgan returned to the office just then. She looked decidedly upset, and though Max seldom showed his feelings, there was a flinty look in his gray eyes, and he replied to Storm's question in a decidedly grim voice.

"Because they found the real jewels where he'd hidden them, before he could get to them, and it appears he'd spent every penny he had on the paste copies. Because he has a history of blaming his misfortunes on the people around him—especially women. Something the authorities over there didn't know until he turned up missing and they found out he'd faked a background good enough to fool their security checks. We do have one break. Paul Galloway is American."

"That's a break?" Morgan said incredulously.

"It'll be easier for us to get information about him quickly," Max explained.

Wolfe had been speaking into the phone softly, and now directed a terse comment to the others. "Keane's checking their computer and the NCIC now."

Jared was looking at Max. "Did your guy at the British Museum know where the bastard's from? Specifically?"

Max hesitated, then said steadily, "Not for sure, no, but he did recall Galloway once mentioning he had some relatives in San Francisco."

Storm, frowning as she leaned back against a wooden filing cabinet, was watching Jared, and when she spoke, her voice was almost absent. "So he might have come back home meaning to go to ground. And who does he see—in one of life's nasty little coincidences?

The woman he blames for ruining his schemes and probably his life. And there hadn't been enough time for him to calm down about it."

It was Morgan who voiced the probability in a flat voice. "Revenge tends to be planned carefully. And it's a drawn-out process, not finished too quickly. He won't kill her, Jared. We have time to find her."

Jared closed his eyes briefly, then opened them and seemed to be looking into some awful place none of the people around him wanted to see for themselves. None of them had to state the obvious, though all of them were thinking about it, just as Jared was torturing himself by thinking about it.

Terrible things could be done to the human body and mind, things that stopped short of killing—but not destroying.

Danica didn't know how long it took her to master the mindless panic; it could have been minutes or hours. At first, she couldn't be still, yet was petrified of moving through the darkness. She took a step away from the wall at her back, terrified of spiders crawling down on her, and found a sensation nearly as bad when the absence of the wall disoriented her even more than the darkness did.

It was so utterly and completely *dark*. Every time she sucked in a gasping breath, she had the nightmarish feeling that the thick darkness contained something evil she was drawing inside her body, something that would choke her. She wrapped her arms around herself, not realizing she was swaying until she half fell back against the wall.

Spiders.

That was when Danica began to get control of herself. Panic was alien to her nature; she had absorbed too many of her father's teachings to discard them now, even under enormous pressure. And she knew only too well that she would be handing the madman upstairs his triumph and his revenge if she allowed him to rule her through her own terror.

So, step by cautious step, she did everything she could to anchor her sanity.

There were no spiders; that was her imagination. She told herself that over and over methodically, remembering how bare the walls and floors had been when the oil lamp had shown them to her. Very bare. Very clean. No ghostly webs.

No spiders.

Keeping the wall at her back, she slid down carefully until she was sitting, her knees drawn up to her chest and her arms wrapped around them. She closed her eyes, because then she could pretend that was the only reason it was dark. She knew very little about meditation, but she knew how to focus her concentration; she thought of a tune she especially liked and began humming it very softly.

By the time she had gone through the song three times, she could feel the calm surrounding her. Good. That was good. Now, still humming automatically, she had to occupy her mind with something so all-consuming it would fill every corner and drive away the darkness.

Unconsciously she smiled.

Jared, naturally. She pictured him in her mind, the way he looked clothed, the way he looked naked. His wonderful eyes, his voice, his passion. She remembered each time they'd made love, the wild frenzy and the aching tenderness. The laughter, the teasing, the gravity, the quiet. Waking in the night to find herself being loved, the darkness velvet then, the intimacy shattering.

A soapy exploration in the shower. A hasty, intense joining on the thick carpet before the fireplace. A primitive mating on sun-warmed grass, their clothing tumbled.

Gradually, as she remembered their time together, Danica realized that what had happened ten years before barely existed for her now. Her father's manipulation was forgiven. The pain was gone. All the regrets had been let go.

That was the past.

Only the present mattered. And the future. There would be a future, of course. There had to be. Because nothing, not Paul Galloway or anything else, could prevent her from doing the one thing her heart demanded.

She had to tell Jared that she had loved him since she was seventeen years old.

"What?" The phone to his ear, Wolfe listened, frowning, his sharp blue eyes lifting to Jared's face. "Yeah, but—all right. Just hurry, will you?"

"Well?" Jared's voice was cracked, hoarse. "What did Keane say? Did he find anything?"

Wolfe nodded. "He thinks he knows the most likely place for Galloway to have taken Dani."

Jared stood up, his face stone, eyes burning. "Where?"

Wolfe stood up as well, though more slowly, his wide shoulders braced as if he expected an attack. "It's an old house, south of here. Belonged to Galloway's aunt. It's been rental property for years, but it's empty now. Or was. Galloway got the key from the agent about a week ago. Keane's on his way, and he knows where the place is."

Jared automatically checked his gun, making sure the clip was full, and then shoved it back into the holster.

"We won't be able to move in for hours, Jared."

He looked across the desk, the stone face cracking. "What?"

Wolfe nodded and went on flatly. "The house is isolated, and there's no cover. Until it gets dark, there's no way we can sneak up on the son-of-a-bitch. If he sees us coming, he could use Dani to hold us off. Or kill her."

Jared moved slightly, as if every muscle in his body rippled in a blind protest against the delay. He wanted to get to Dani, *had* to, and every second he wasn't doing something to get her back was raw torture. He wanted to roar out his pain and rage, wanted to hit something—and judging from his wary stillness, Wolfe obviously expected it to be him.

Shoot the messenger of bad news, Jared thought somewhat wildly. Hit him, at least. God, it was tempting. He felt more than heard a shifting behind him, and knew without looking that Max had taken a step toward him. They were all watching him, all waiting for him to explode, and he wondered vaguely what his face looked like to make them so apprehensive.

But then he felt a sensation unlike anything he'd ever felt before. It was a kind of calm, of peace, not his, yet wrapping around him like a comforting blanket. And he heard . . . very faintly . . . an elusive but familiar tune. As if someone were humming softly.

"It's her song," he murmured, not even aware of speaking aloud. Dani's song, her favorite. She hummed it often while working, and had explained to him that it helped her concentrate. A lovely song, from a Broadway musical . . .

"Jared?"

He turned his head slowly and looked at Max. He felt very calm. "She's all right," he said quietly.

Max nodded, and one of his rare smiles softened his hard face and lightened the gray eyes. "Good."

No one voiced the thought that even if he knew somehow, Danica might not *stay* all right during the coming hours. They merely waited silently for Keane Tyler to arrive.

Danica seldom wore a watch and wasn't wearing one now; she wondered if that were a good or a bad thing. Time passed, she knew that. She had hummed her favorite song over and over, complete from first note to last, so she thought hours had probably passed. She kept her eyes closed, turning her head to rest her cheek against her knee.

She thought about Jared.

There was no logical reason to expect him to find her. How could he know about Paul Galloway? With his mind intent on the Bannister collection, he would likely assume that was why she'd been snatched. But the collection had already been moved to the museum, its transfer trumpeted publicly, so perhaps that would give Jared pause.

He'd be worried, she thought, probably frantic.

Still humming softly, she tried to reach out, tried to tell Jared she was all right. It was terribly important to her that he know that. She wasn't sure if she was successful, since she'd never tried anything like this before, but she thought if it was indeed possible to touch another, beloved mind, then Jared would know she was all right.

She might have dozed. Cramped, she stood up shakily and flexed her limbs, pressing against the wall like a runner stretching before a race. She kept her eyes closed most of the time, because opening them was like opening the door and allowing fear to trickle in. When the cramps had eased, she settled back down on the hard floor.

She might have dozed again. The sudden sounds from upstairs brought her head jerking up, and her arms tightened around her legs as she strained to listen. There'd been a crash, like a window breaking, heavy thuds against the floor above her head, and what might have been a gunshot.

Then there was another kind of crash, like a door yanked nearly off its hinges, and rapid footsteps on the creaky wooden stairs.

"Dani?"

She opened her eyes then, blinking at the light spilling down the stairs from above. He was coming toward her, silhouetted by the light, and she felt the most incredible sense of elation when he pulled her up into his arms.

"Dani," he muttered hoarsely into her hair.

Sliding her arms around his lean waist, she murmured his name in return, and then added dreamily, "What kept you?"

NINE

"For all the world as if you never doubted I'd come," Jared said long after midnight as they lay close together in their lamplit bed.

"I never did." She snuggled even closer to his side, her slim fingers toying with the thick dark hair on his chest. "I mean, I couldn't imagine how you'd know to look for an enemy in *my* past rather than someone after the collection, but that didn't matter. I was sure you'd find me."

Jared's arms tightened around her. "Finding you was relatively easy once we knew who to look for. Galloway hadn't exactly covered his tracks. But getting into that house quickly enough so he wouldn't have time to hurt you took a bit of planning."

Danica lifted her head from his shoulder and looked down at him gravely. "It's a miracle one of you didn't get killed, going through the windows like that. I saw you thanking Keane and Wolfe later. Did I get the wrong impression, or are things a bit less tense between you and Wolfe?"

"A bit." He smiled up at her. "I now have a much better understanding of what it did to him to have Storm in danger—which was partly my fault. And since he was the one to pull me off Galloway before I could kill the bastard, I suppose I owe him for that."

"Well, of course you do," she said severely. "What kind of honeymoon would we have if you spent the whole time in trouble for acting like a cop out of your jurisdiction?"

He had reached up to stroke her cheek, and his hand stilled against her face. "Honeymoon?"

"I realize you're obligated to stay in San Francisco until your trap catches Nightshade," she said, keeping her voice very calm and matter-of-fact. "But I really think we should go ahead and get married. It's not that I mind living in sin, you understand, it's just that—"

"Dani?"

"Hmmm?"

"Are you trying to tell me you love me?" His voice was calm, but the undercurrent of strain was conspicuous.

She smiled at him gently. "Love you? I fell in love with you when I was seventeen years old. And when I heard your name eleven years later, and turned to see you standing there, I knew I'd never stopped loving you."

His hand slid around to her nape and he pulled her down far enough to kiss her. His mouth was shaking, and his voice shook when he said, "God, Dani, I love you so much. . . . I wanted to tell you every minute we were together, but I didn't want to overwhelm you the way I did the first time."

"I know," she murmured. "It was something I thought about in the cellar, because I wanted so much to tell you how I felt about you. I realized you hadn't said anything because you were so determined not to make the same mistakes this time."

He framed her face with both hands, those intense eyes vibrant in the lamplight. "I couldn't take a chance of losing you again," he said huskily. "I was pretty sure you knew we belonged together as much as I did, and God knows we couldn't be near each other without making love—but you never seemed to want to talk about the future."

"I had to let go of the past first."

Jared nodded. "Dani . . . are you sure? I mean, about marriage. I'd be willing to wait, if you need more time."

"Do you want to wait?"

He moved suddenly, rolling so that she was on her back and he was raised above her. "No. I'd drag you out to find a preacher tonight if I could." He kissed her, first tenderly and then with building hunger.

When he finally lifted his head, Danica smiled and murmured, "I don't want to wait either. I love you,

Jared. I want to be your wife. *Really* be your wife, this time."

He kissed her again. "And this time I promise to really be a husband, sweetheart."

"Then how soon can we find a preacher?" she asked solemnly.

"The preacher isn't the problem—establishing residency is. But Max said he'd be happy to pull a few strings. How would you feel about getting married just as soon as we can get the blood tests?"

Danica wreathed her arms around his neck and demonstrated her enthusiasm for the suggestion. It was quite a long time later before either of them could speak coherently again, and when they could, her voice was soft.

"I love you, Jared."

"I love you, too, sweetheart."

She lifted her head from his shoulder and smiled down at him very gently. "Enough to tell me the whole truth about *Mysteries Past* and this trap of yours?"

He groaned softly, but he was smiling. It wasn't so much to ask, he thought. Besides that, he hated keeping secrets from the love of his life.

"Start it—once upon a time," she suggested.

Laughing, he did.

It was long after midnight, but Morgan wasn't ready for sleep. It had been a very tense and eventful day, and even though things had ended happily for all concerned—except Galloway, who didn't count—Morgan found that she simply couldn't relax. She puttered around the apartment, listening to the late news on television while she washed a few bits of delicate crystal in the kitchen sink and then wandered back to the living room.

Oddly enough, she wasn't at all surprised to see him standing there, much as he had the night he'd been wounded. Except that he wasn't wounded now, or masked. And his lean, handsome face was, she thought, uncharacteristically strained.

"Good evening," she said dryly.

He waited until she crossed the room to stand before him, and when he spoke, it was quickly. "I never really thanked you for taking care of me, Morgana."

"Is that why you're here?"

"Reason enough, I think."

"You're welcome."

Quinn eyed her with faint exasperation. "You don't make it easy for me," he told her.

Morgan smiled slightly. "Oh, I see—you want me to make it *easy* for you. Why should I?"

He cleared his throat. "Do both of us know what we're talking about?" he wondered.

"Yes. We're talking about the fact that I more or less offered myself to you that last night, and you bolted so fast you practically left your boots behind."

A little smile curved his mouth. "The image that

conjures, Morgana, is hardly flattering. To either of us."

"I agree. Is that why you came back here? Because you had second thoughts?"

Quinn hesitated, then shook his head. "No, you were obviously not in your right mind at the time."

"I wasn't?" She put her hands on her hips and stared up at him. "Are you trying to save me from myself, Alex?"

"Something like that," he murmured.

"Then why did you come back here?"

"To thank you, that's all."

Morgan decided to take off the gloves; this sparring, she thought, had gone on long enough. "Make love to me," she said softly.

Quinn stiffened. "You don't know what you're saying." His voice was even, but his hands slowly bunched into fists at his sides.

"What's the cliché? Live today, for tomorrow we may die?"

"That's no reason to deliberately make a mistake," he responded a bit tautly. "And it would be a mistake, Morgana. Never doubt that."

"Because you're Quinn?" They hadn't talked about this when he'd been recovering there, and she had a peculiar idea that was really why he'd come back— because he wanted her to understand fully who and what he was.

"Isn't that reason enough? Name any major city

in the Western world, and the cops there want me behind bars at the very least. That won't change, no matter how this turns out. I'm too effective to go public, and Interpol knows it. They've got me by the—short hairs." He laughed, honest amusement in the sound. "I can't complain. I had a hell of a dance, and now I have to pay the band."

"Extend the metaphor." She smiled faintly. "The music hasn't stopped, the tune's just changed. You enjoy the dance, Alex. And Interpol knows that. So they changed the music for you."

"And made sure I'd dance for them?" He laughed again. "Probably." His voice and face became abruptly expressionless. "The point is that . . . I'm never going to be respectable, Morgana. I don't want to be. You're right; I *enjoy* this dance. I don't feel a bit of regret about my past."

"But they caught you," she murmured.

He nodded. "They caught me. They could have locked me up; instead they gave me a choice. And I chose. I'll keep my bargain with them. I'll dance to their tune. As you said—only the music's changed; the dance is just as much fun."

"You won't be able to steal for yourself," she noted, watching him with an expression of mild interest.

He shrugged carelessly. "The proceeds of my past will see me through even a long future in style, sweet."

In a thoughtful tone, she said, "I would have

expected them to demand you return those proceeds."

"They tried." He smiled sardonically. "I told them I'd forget how to dance."

Placidly she said, "You are a complete villain, aren't you?"

Quinn eyed her a bit warily. "I don't know why on earth it's so," he commented, "but I have the most insane urge to insist that I am, in fact, just that."

"And selfish and egotistical and reckless. Without morals, scruples, compassion, or shame. Lawless, heartless, wicked, and rebellious. How am I doing?"

"Just fine," he answered with a suggestion of gritted teeth.

She nodded seriously. "Let's see. . . . You're a thief of world renown, there's no doubt of that. You've quite cheerfully broken a number of the laws of God and man. Without, according to you, one iota of remorse. And you're on the right side of the law now only because it was infinitely preferable to spending the remainder of your life in a prison cell."

"All true," he said grimly.

"Do you also kick puppies and steal candy from children?"

Quinn drew a deep breath. "Only on odd Thursdays."

She smiled a little. "You know, I'd have a much easier time believing all these rotten things about you if you didn't try so hard to make me believe them."

With a glint of despair in his vivid eyes, he said, "Morgan, get it through your head—I'm not a nice person."

"I never said you were."

Quinn blinked, but recovered quickly. "I get it. You're a danger junkie, that's why you brazenly invited me to be your lover."

"No," she answered seriously, "that's why I want to get involved with your work. Getting involved with your body is another matter entirely."

He crossed his arms over his broad chest suddenly in the curiously controlled movement of a man who suspects he's about to go totally berserk. "You're an absurd woman, you know that?" he said carefully.

She lifted an eyebrow at him. "Alex, you can't expect me to believe you're an evil ogre when you won't even let yourself be decently seduced."

Quinn bowed his head and muttered a string of soft but heartfelt oaths.

Morgan kept her expression grave with an effort. "Look, I'm not an idiot. You've broken the law, frequently and with a certain amount of panache. Being a law-abiding person myself, I find that hard to excuse. I can't even console myself by believing that some tragedy led you into a life of crime in the best melodramatic tradition. You enjoyed your past, and you're enjoying this dangerous shell game now.

"I've told myself all that. I've been very rational about the situation. I know all the odds are against me.

Any woman who gets involved with you is asking for trouble. She's also asking for heartache—not because you're an evil man, but because you aren't."

Quinn raised his head and stared at her.

Her fleeting amusement gone, Morgan smiled a bit ruefully. "I've tried. I have tried. But I can't seem to do much about this. Except try to keep my head. You'd be damnably easy to love, Alex. Rogues always are, and you're certainly that. But I'm not fool enough to believe I could catch the wind in my hands. I don't want golden rings or bedroom promises. And I won't make it difficult for you. I won't even ask you to say good-bye when it's over."

"Dammit, would you stop—"

"Being noble?" she interrupted, her dry voice cutting through his rough one. "Isn't that what you've been doing?"

After a moment, he said, "I don't want to hurt you."

"I know. And you certainly get nine out of ten for effort."

The light comment didn't alter his grim expression. "Ten out of ten, because it stops here." Each word was bitten off sharply with the sound of finality. "If you want to play in the danger zone, pick some other rogue to show you how."

Morgan gazed at the spot where he'd stood long after he was gone. Then, gradually, she began smiling. Things were, she decided cheerfully, definitely looking up.

AUTHOR'S NOTE

I hope you've enjoyed *The Trouble with Jared*, the third story in my *Men of Mysteries Past* series for Loveswept.

Next, and finally, is ALL FOR QUINN, in which our infamous cat burglar makes a risky decision that will bring him one step closer to the deadly thief known as Nightshade, and propel Quinn and Morgan into a situation full of surprises and dangers for both of them.

THE EDITOR'S CORNER

July belongs to ONLY DADDY—and six magnificent heroes who discover romance, family style! Whether he's a confirmed bachelor or a single father, a small-town farmer or a big-city cop, each of these men can't resist the pitter-patter of little feet. And when he falls under the spell of that special woman's charms, he'll stop at nothing to claim her as a partner in parenting and passion. . . .

Leading the terrific line-up for July is Linda Cajio with **ME AND MRS. JONES**, LOVESWEPT #624. Actually, it should be *ex*-Mrs. Jones since high school sweethearts Kate Perry and Mitch Jones have been divorced for eleven years, after an elopement and a disastrous brief marriage. Now Kate is back in town, and Mitch, who's always been able to talk her into just about anything, persuades her to adopt a wise-eyed injured tomcat, with the promise that he'd be making plenty of house calls! Not sure she can play stepmother to his daughter Chelsea, Kate tells herself to run from the man who so easily ignites her desire, but she still remembers his hands on her body and can't send him away. To Mitch, no memory can ever match the heat of their passion, and he's been waiting all this time to reclaim the only woman he's ever truly loved. With fire in his touch, he sets about convincing her to let him in once more, and this time he intends to keep her in his arms for always. An utterly delightful story from beginning to end, told with Linda's delicious sense of humor and sensitive touch.

In **RAISING HARRY,** LOVESWEPT #625 by Victoria Leigh, Griff Ross is a single father coping with the usual problems of raising a high-spirited three-year-old son. He's never been jealous of Harry until he finds him in the arms of their neighbor Sharron Capwell. Her lush mouth makes Griff long to kiss her breathless, while her soft curves tempt him with visions of bare shoulders touched only by moonlight and his hands. She makes him burn with pleasure as no woman ever has, but Griff, still hurt by a betrayal he's never forgiven, insists he wants only a friend and a lover. Single and childless, Sharron has always been content with her life—until she thrills to the ecstasy Griff shows her, and now finds herself struggling with her need to be his wife and Harry's mother. Rest assured that a happily-ever-after awaits these two, as well as the young one, once they admit the love they can't deny. Victoria tells a compelling love story, one you won't be able to put down.

Who can resist **THE COURTING COWBOY,** LOVESWEPT #626 by Glenna McReynolds? Ty Garrett is a rough-edged rancher who wants a woman to share the seasons, to love under the Colorado skies. But he expects that finding a lady in his middle-of-nowhere town would be very rough—until a spirited visiting teacher fascinates his son and captivates him too! Victoria Willoughby has beautiful skin, a very kissable mouth, and a sensual innocence that beckons Ty to woo her with fierce, possessive passion. He awakens her to pleasures she's never imagined, teaches her how wonderful taking chances can be, and makes her feel alluring, wanton. But she's already let one man rule her life and she's vowed never to belong to anyone ever again. Still, she knows that finding Ty is a miracle; now if she'll only realize that he's the best man and the right man for her . . . Glenna's talent shines brightly in this terrific romance.

Bonnie Pega begins her deliciously sexy novel, **THEN COMES MARRIAGE**, LOVESWEPT #627, with the hero and heroine meeting in a very unlikely place. Single mother-to-be Libby Austin certainly thinks that seeing the hunk of her dreams in a childbirth class is truly rotten luck, but she breathes a sigh of relief when she discovers that Zac Webster is coaching his sister-in-law, not his wife! His potent masculinity can charm every stitch of clothing off a woman's body; too bad he makes it all too clear that a child doesn't fit into his life. Still, unable to resist the temptation of Libby's blue velvet eyes and delectable smile, Zac lays siege to her senses, and her response of torrential kisses and fevered caresses drive him even wilder with hunger. Libby has given him more than he's hoped for—and a tricky dilemma. Can a man who's sworn off marriage and vows he's awful with kids claim a wildfire bride and her baby? With this wonderful romance, her second LOVESWEPT, Bonnie proves that she's a name to watch for.

There's no sexier **MAN AROUND THE HOUSE** than the hero in Cindy Gerard's upcoming LOVESWEPT, #628. Matthew Spencer is a lean, muscled heartbreaker, and when he answers his new next-door neighbor's cries for help, he finds himself rescuing disaster-prone Katie

McDonald, who's an accident waiting to happen—and a sassy temptress who's sure to keep him up nights. Awakening his hunger with the speed of a summer storm, Katie senses his pain and longs to comfort him, but Matthew makes her feel too much, makes her want more than she can have. Though she lets herself dare to dream of being loved, Katie knows she's all wrong for a man who's walking a careful path to regain custody of his son. He needs nice and normal, not her kind of wild and reckless—no matter that they sizzle in each other's arms. But Matthew's not about to give up a woman who adores his child, listens to his favorite golden oldie rock station, and gives him kisses that knock his socks off and make the stars spin. The magic of Cindy's writing shines through in this enchanting tale of love.

Finishing the line-up in a big way is Marcia Evanick and **IN DADDY'S ARMS,** LOVESWEPT #629. Brave enough to fight back from wounds inflicted in the line of duty, Bain O'Neill is devastated when doctors tell him he'll never be a father. Having a family is the only dream that ever mattered to him, a fantasy he can't give up, not when he knows that somewhere there are two children who are partly his, the result of an anonymous sperm donation he made years ago. A little investigation helps him locate his daughters—and their mother, Erin Flynn, a fiery-haired angel who tastes as good as she looks. Widowed for two years, Erin takes his breath away and heals him with her loving touch. Bain hates keeping the truth from her, and though the children soon beg him to be their daddy, he doesn't dare confess his secret to Erin, not until he's silenced her doubts about his love and makes her believe he's with her to stay forever. All the stirring emotions and funny touches that you've come to expect from Marcia are in this fabulous story.

On sale this month from Bantam are three spectacular women's novels. Dianne Edouard and Sandra Ware have teamed up once again and written **SACRED LIES,** a spellbinding novel of sin, seduction, and betrayal. Romany Chase is the perfect spy: intelligent, beautiful, a woman who thrills to the hunt. But with her latest mission, Romany is out of her depth. Adrift in a world where redemption may arrive too late, she is torn between the enigmatic priest she has orders to seduce and the fierce agent she desires. Beneath the glittering Roman moon, a deadly conspiracy of greed, corruption, and shattering evil is closing in, and Romany must choose whom to believe—and whom to love.

With more than several million copies of her novels in print, Kay Hooper is indisputably one of the best loved and popular authors of romantic fiction—and now she has penned **THE WIZARD OF SEATTLE,** a fabulous, magical story of immortal love and mesmerizing fantasy. Serena Smyth travels cross-country to Seattle to find Richard Patrick Merlin, guided by an instinct born of her determination to become a master wizard like him. She knows he can be her teacher, but she never expects the fire he ignites in her body and soul. Their love forbidden by an ancient law, Serena and Merlin will take a desperate gamble and travel to the long-lost world of Atlantis—to change the history that threatens to keep them apart for eternity.

From bestselling author Susan Johnson comes **SILVER FLAME,** the steamy sequel about the Braddock-Black dynasty you read about in **BLAZE.** Pick up a copy and find out why *Romantic Times* gave the author its Best Sensual Historical Romance Award. Sizzling with electrifying sensuality, **SILVER FLAME** burns hot! When Empress

Jordan is forced to sell her most precious possession to the highest bidder in order to feed her brothers and sisters, Trey Braddock-Black knows he must have her, no matter what the cost. The half-Absarokee rogue has no intention of settling down with one woman, but once he's spent three weeks with the sweet enchantress, he knows he can never give her up. . . .

Also on sale this month, in the hardcover edition from Doubleday, is **THE PAINTED LADY,** the stunningly sensual debut novel by Lucia Grahame. All of Paris and London recognize Fleur not only as Frederick Brooks's wife, but also as the successful painter's most inspiring model. But few know the secrets behind his untimely death and the terrible betrayal that leaves Fleur with a heart of ice—and no choice but to accept Sir Anthony Camwell's stunning offer: a fortune to live on in return for five nights of unrestrained surrender to what he plans to teach her—the exquisite art of love.

Happy reading!

With warmest wishes,

Nita Taublib

Nita Taublib
Associate Publisher
LOVESWEPT and FANFARE

Don't miss these exciting
books by your favorite
Bantam authors
On Sale in May:

SACRED LIES
by Dianne Edouard
and Sandra Ware

THE WIZARD OF SEATTLE
by Kay Hooper

SILVER FLAME
by Susan Johnson

"SPECIAL SNEAK PREVIEW"
THE MAGNIFICENT ROGUE
by Iris Johansen
On Sale in August

SACRED LIES
by Dianne Edouard and Sandra Ware

On Sale in May

Romany Chase is the perfect spy: intelligent, beautiful, a woman who thrills to the hunt. But torn between the fierce Israeli agent she desires and the enigmatic priest she has orders to seduce, Romany is out of her depth—adrift in a world where redemption may arrive too late . . . .

As soon as Romany opened the door, she knew she wasn't alone. Someone waited for her. Somewhere in the apartment.

She had never carried a gun. There had never been a need. Even though Sully could have gotten her easy clearance, and had more than once urged her to take along some insurance. But her assignments never warranted it. Except that one time, in Geneva, and that situation had come totally out of left field.

She allowed her eyes to become adjusted to the gloom and, easing herself against the wall, moved to the edge of the living room. She searched the shadows. Strained to see something behind the thick lumps and bumps of furniture. Nothing. She crouched lower and inched closer to the door opening into her bedroom.

She peered around the corner. Whoever was in the apartment had switched on the ceiling fan and the small lamp that sat on a dressing table in the adjoining bath. The soft light cast the room in semidarkness, and she could make out the large solid shape of a man. He reclined easily upon her bed, a marshmallowy heap of pillows propped against his back. He hadn't bothered to draw back the covers, and he lay on top of the spread completely naked.

She should have run, gotten out of her apartment as quickly as possible. Except she recognized the hard muscles under the deeply tanned skin, the black curling hair, the famous smirk that passed for a smile. Recognized the man who was a cold-blooded killer—and her lover.

Romany moved through the doorway and smiled. "I'm not even going to ask how you got in here, David."

She heard his dark laugh. "Is that any way to greet an old friend?"

She walked farther into the room and stood by the side of the bed. She stared into the bright green eyes, still a surprise after all this time. But then everything about David ben Haar was a surprise. "Why don't you make yourself comfortable?"

"I am . . . almost." He reached for her hand and ran it slowly down his chest, stopping just short of the black hair at his groin.

She glanced down, focusing on her hand, pale and thin clasped inside his. She could hear her breath catch inside her throat. And as if that sound had been meant as some sort of signal, he pulled her down beside him.

She rested with her back against him, letting him work the muscles at her shoulders, brush his lips against her hair. She didn't turn when she finally decided to speak. "What are you doing here, David?"

"I came to see you." The words didn't sound like a complete lie.

She twisted herself round to look up at him. "That's terribly flattering, David, but it won't work."

She watched the smirk almost stretch into a real smile.

"Okay, I came to make sure that Sully is taking good care of my girl."

"I'm not your girl, David." She tried not to sound mean, or hurt, or anything. But she could feel the muscles of his stomach tighten against her back.

"You know Sully's a fucking asshole," he said finally. "What's he waiting on, those jerks to open up a concentration camp and gas a few thousand Jews?"

"David, Sully's not an asshole. . . . Hey, what in the hell do you mean?" She jerked around, waiting for an answer, watching his eyes turn cold.

"Gimme a break, Romany."

"Dammit, David, I don't have the slightest idea what you're talking about. Besides, what in the hell have concentration camps got to do with . . . ?" She stopped short, not willing to play her hand, even though David probably knew all the cards she was holding.

"Well, Romany, I can save you, and Sully, and all your little friends over at the CIA a whole helluva lotta trouble. Somebody—and I think you're deaf, dumb, and blind if you haven't pegged who that is—is stealing the Church blind, swiping paintings right off the museum walls, then slipping by some pretty goddamn good fakes."

She watched him stare at her from inside the darkness of her bed, waiting with that flirting smirk on his mouth for her to say something. But she didn't answer.

" . . . And the SOB at the other end of this operation"—he was finishing what he'd started—"whether your CIA geniuses want to admit it or not, is black-marketing the genuine articles, funneling the profits to a group of neo-Nazis who aren't going to settle for German reunification."

"Neo-Nazis?"

She could hear him grit his teeth. "Yeah, neo-Nazis. Getting East and West Germany together was just the first stage of their nasty little operation. They've got big plans, Romany. But they're the same old fuckers. Just a little slicker."

"David, I can't believe—"

"Shit, you people never want to believe—"

"Stop it, David."

He dropped his head and took in a deep staccatoed breath. She felt his hands move up her arms to her shoulders and force her body close to his. "Sorry, Romany." He sounded hoarse. Then suddenly she felt him laughing against her. "You know something"—he was drawing back—"you're on the wrong side, Romany. We wouldn't have these stupid fights if you'd come and work with me. With the Mossad."

"Yeah? Work with you, huh? And just what inducement can you offer, David ben Haar?" She pulled away from him and stood up.

Her feelings about David were a tangled mess—which, after she'd watched him board the plane for Tel Aviv thirteen months ago, she'd thought she could safely leave unwound. But here he was again, still looking at her with that quizzical twist to his lips that she couldn't help but read as a challenge.

She wanted his hands on her. That was the thought that kept repeating itself, blotting out everything else in her mind. Her own hands trembled as she pushed the hair away from her neck and began to undo the buttons at her back. Undressing for him slowly, the way he liked it.

She hadn't let herself know how much she'd missed this, until she was beneath the covers naked beside him, and his hands were really on her again, taking control, his mouth moving everywhere on her body. The pulse of the ceiling fan blended suddenly with the rush of blood in her ears, and David's heat was under her skin like fire.

She pressed herself closer against him, her need for him blocking out her doubts. She wanted his solidness, his back under her hands, the hardness of him along the length of her body. David ben Haar, the perfect sexual fantasy. But real. Flesh and blood with eyes green as the sea. She looked into his eyes as he pulled her beneath him. There was no lightness in them now, only the same intensity of passion as when he killed. He came into her hard, and she shut her eyes, matching her rhythm to his. To dream was all right, as long as you didn't let it go beyond the borders of your bed.

*   *   *

With one small edge of the curtain rolled back, David ben Haar could just see through the balcony railing where the red Alfa Romeo Spider was waiting to park in the street. Romany had been flying about the apartment when the car had first driven up, still cursing him for her half-damp hair, amusingly anxious to keep the priest from getting as far as her door.

"I could hide in the bedroom." He had said it from his comfortable position, lying still naked on her sofa. Laughing at her as she went past buttoning her dress, hobbling on one shoe back to the bedroom.

"I don't trust you, David ben Haar." She'd come back with her other shoe and was throwing a hairbrush into that satchel she called a purse.

"Romany?" He had concentrated on the intent face, the wild curls threatening to break loose from the scarf that bound them. "Morrow one of the bad guys?"

Picking up a sweater, she had looked over at him then, with something remarkably like guilt. "I don't know." She was going for the door. "That's what I'm supposed to find out."

Then she was gone, her heels rat-tatting down the stairs. High heels at Villa d'Este. Just like an American. They never took anything seriously, then covered it up with a cynicism they hadn't earned. Romany was the flip side of that, of course, all earnestness and innocence. She was smart and she had guts. But it wouldn't be enough to protect her. He got up.

As he watched now, the Spider was swinging into the parking space that had finally become available at the curb. The door opened and a man got out, turning to where Romany had just emerged from under the balcony overhang. The man didn't exactly match the car, he looked far too American. What he didn't look like was a priest.

He watched them greet each other. Very friendly. The compressor on the air conditioner picked that minute to kick in again, so he couldn't hope to hear what was said. The man opened the passenger door for her, then walked around to get in. They didn't pull out right away, and he was wondering why when he saw the canvas top go down. The engine roared up as they shot away from the curb. He could tell by the tilt of her head that Romany was laughing.

They had not spoken for some time now, standing among the tall cypress, looking out below to the valley. The dying sun had painted everything in a kind of saturated light, and he seemed almost surreal standing next to her, his fair aureole of hair and tall body in light-colored shirt and slacks glowing against the blackness of the trees.

They had played today, she and Julian Morrow. Like happy strangers who had met in Rome, with no history and no future. She had felt it immediately, the playfulness, implicit in the red car, in the way he wore the light, casual clothes. Like an emblem, like a costume at a party.

She had sat in the red car, letting the wind blow everything away from her mind, letting it rip David from her body. Forgetting the job. Forgetting that the man beside her was a priest and a suspect, and she a paid agent of the United States government.

They had played today. And she had liked this uncomplicated persona better than any he had so far let her see. Liked his ease and his sense of humor, and the pleasure he had seemed to find in their joyful sharing of this place. She had to stop playing now, but this was the Julian Morrow she must hold in her mind. Not the priest. Not the suspect in criminal forgery. But a Julian Morrow to whom she could want to make love.

He turned to her and smiled. For a moment the truth of her treachery rose to stick in her throat. But she forced it down. This was her job. She was committed.

She smiled back, moving closer, as if she might want a better view, or perhaps some little shelter from the wind. He must have thought the latter, because she felt his hands draping her sweater more firmly around her shoulders.

Time to take the advantage. And shifting backward, she pressed herself lightly against his chest, her eyes closed. She was barely breathing, feeling for any answering strain. But she could find no sense of any rejection in his posture.

She turned. He was looking down at her. His eyes, so close, were unreadable. She would never remember exactly what had happened next, but she knew when her arms went around him. And the small moment of her triumph when she felt him hard against her. Then she was pulling him down toward her, her fingers tangling in his hair, her mouth moving on his.

At the moment when she ceased thinking at all, he let her go, suddenly, with a gesture almost brutal that set her tumbling back. His hand reached for her wrist, didn't let her fall. But the grip was not kind or gentle.

His face was closed. Completely. Anger would have been better. She was glad when he turned away from her, walking back in the direction of the car. There would be no dinner tonight at the wonderful terraced restaurant he had talked about today. Of that she was perfectly sure. It was going to be a long drive back to Rome.

THE WIZARD OF SEATTLE
the unique new romantic fantasy from
Kay Hooper

On Sale in May

In the bestselling tradition of the time-travel romances of Diana Gabaldon and Constance O'Day-Flannery, Kay Hooper creates her own fabulous, magical story of timeless love and mesmerizing fantasy.

She looked like a ragged, storm-drenched urchin, but from the moment Serena Smyth appeared on his Seattle doorstep Richard Patrick Merlin recognized the spark behind her green eyes, the wild talent barely held in check. And he would help her learn to control her gift, despite a taboo so ancient that the reasons for its existence had been forgotten. But he never suspected that in his rebellion he would risk all he had and all he was to feel a love none of his kind had ever known.

Seattle, 1984

It was his home. She knew that, although where her certainty came from was a mystery to her. Like the inner tug that had drawn her across the country to find him, the knowledge seemed instinctive, beyond words or reason. She didn't even know his name. But she knew what he was. He was what she wanted to be, needed to be, what all her instincts insisted she had to be, and only he could teach her what she needed to learn.

Until this moment, she had never doubted that he would accept her as his pupil. At sixteen, she was passing through that stage of development experienced by humans, twice in their lifetimes, a stage marked by total self-absorption and the unshakable certainty that the entire universe revolves around oneself. It occurred in infancy and in adolescence, but rarely ever again, unless one were utterly unconscious of reality. Those traits had given her the confidence she had needed in order to cross the country alone with no more than a ragged backpack and a few dollars.

But they deserted her now, as she stood at the wrought iron gates and stared up at the secluded old Victorian house. The rain beat down on her, and lightning flashed in the stormy sky, illuminating the turrets and gables of the house; there were few lighted windows, and those were dim rather than welcoming.

It *looked* like the home of a wizard.

She almost ran, abruptly conscious of her aloneness. But then she squared her thin shoulders, shoved open the gate, and walked steadily to the front door. Ignoring the bell, she used the brass knocker to rap sharply. The knocker was fashioned in the shape of an owl, the creature that symbolized wisdom, a familiar of wizards throughout fiction.

She didn't know about fact.

Her hand was shaking, and she gave it a fierce frown as she rapped the knocker once more against the solid door. She barely had time to release the knocker before the door was pulled open.

Tall and physically powerful, his raven hair a little shaggy and his black eyes burning with an inner fire, he surveyed the dripping, ragged girl on his doorstep with lofty disdain for long moments during which all of her determination melted away to nothing. Then he caught her collar with one elegant hand, much as he might have grasped a stray cat, and yanked her into the well-lit entrance hall. He studied her with daunting sternness.

What he saw was an almost painfully thin girl who looked much younger than her sixteen years. Her threadbare clothing was soaked; her short, tangled hair was so wet that only a hint of its normal vibrant red color was apparent; and her small face—all angles and seemingly filled with huge eyes—was white and pinched. She was no more attractive than a stray mongrel pup.

"Well?"

The vast poise of sixteen years deserted the girl as he barked the one word in her ear. She gulped. "I—I want to be a wizard," she managed finally, defiantly.

"Why?"

She was soaked to the skin, tired, hungry, and possessed a temper that had more than once gotten her into trouble. Her green eyes snapping, she glared up into his handsome, expressionless face, and her voice lost all its timidity.

"I *will* be a wizard! If you won't teach me, I'll find someone who will. I can summon fire already—a little—and I can *feel* the power inside me. All I need is a teacher, and I'll be great one day—"

He lifted her clear off the floor and shook her briefly, effortlessly, inducing silence with no magic at all. "The first lesson an apprentice must learn," he told her calmly, "is to never—ever—shout at a Master."

Then he casually released her, conjured a bundle of clothing out of thin air, and handed it to her. Then he waved a hand negligently and sent her floating up the dark stairs toward a bathroom.

And so it began.

Seattle, Present

His fingers touched her breasts, stroking soft skin and teasing the hard pink nipples. The swollen weight filled his hands as he lifted and kneaded, and when she moaned and arched her back, he lowered his mouth to her. He stopped thinking.

He felt. He felt his own body, taut and pulsing with desire, the blood hot in his veins. He felt her body, soft and warm and willing. He felt her hand on him, stroking slowly, her touch hungry and assured. Her moans and sighs filled his ears, and the heat of her need rose until her flesh burned. The tension inside him coiled more tightly, making his body ache, until he couldn't stand to wait another moment. He sank his flesh into hers, feeling her legs close strongly about his hips. Expertly, lustfully, she met his thrusts, undulating beneath him, her female body the cradle all men returned to. The heat between them built until it was a fever raging out of control, until his body was gripped by the inescapable, inexorable drive for release and pounded frantically inside her. Then, at last, the heat and tension drained from him in a rush . . .

Serena sat bolt upright in bed, gasping. In shock, she stared across the darkened room for a moment, and then she hurriedly leaned over and turned on the lamp on the nightstand. Blinking in the light, she held her hands up and stared at them, reassuring herself that they were hers, still slender and pale and tipped with neat oval nails.

They were hers. She was here and unchanged. Awake. Aware. Herself again.

She could still feel the alien sensations, still see the powerful bronzed hands against paler, softer skin, and still feel sensations her body was incapable of experiencing simply because she was female, not male—

And then she realized.

"Dear God . . . Richard," she whispered.

She had been inside his mind, somehow, in his head just like before, and he had been with another woman. He had been having sex with another woman. Serena had felt what he felt, from the sensual enjoyment of soft female flesh under his touch to the ultimate draining pleasure of orgasm. *She had felt what he felt.*

She drew her knees up and hugged them, feeling tears burning her eyes and nausea churning in her stomach. Another woman. He had a woman somewhere, and she wasn't new because there had been a sense of familiarity in him, a certain knowledge. He knew this woman. Her skin was familiar, her taste, her desire. His body knew hers.

Even Master wizards, it seemed, had appetites just like other men.

Serena felt a wave of emotions so powerful she could endure them only in silent anguish. Her thoughts were tangled and fierce and raw. Not a monk, no, hardly a monk. In fact, it appeared he was quite a proficient lover, judging by the woman's response to him.

On her nightstand, the lamp's bulb burst with a violent sound, but she neither heard it nor noticed the return of darkness to the room.

So he was just a man after all, damn him, a man who got horny like other men and went to some woman who'd spread her legs for him. And often. His trips "out of town" were more frequent these last years. Oh, horny indeed . . .

Unnoticed by Serena, her television set flickered to life, madly scanned though all the channels, and then died with a sound as apologetic as a muffled cough.

Damn him. What'd he do, keep a mistress? Some pretty, pampered blonde—she had been blond, naturally—with empty hot eyes who wore slinky nightgowns and crotchless panties, and moaned like a bitch in heat? Was there only one? Or had he bedded a succession of women over the years, keeping his reputation here in Seattle all nice and tidy while he satisfied his appetites elsewhere?

Serena heard a little sound, and was dimly shocked to realize it came from her throat. It sounded like that of an animal in pain, some tortured creature hunkered down in the dark as it waited helplessly to find out if it would live or die. She didn't realize that she was rocking gently. She didn't see her alarm clock flash a series of red numbers before going dark, or notice that her stereo system was spitting out tape from a cassette.

Only when the overhead light suddenly exploded was Serena jarred from her misery. With a tremendous effort, she struggled to control herself.

"Concentrate," she whispered. "Concentrate. Find the switch." And, for the first time, perhaps spurred on by her urgent need to control what she felt, she did find it. Her wayward energies stopped swirling all around her and were instantly drawn into some part of her she'd never recognized before, where they were completely and safely contained, held there in waiting without constant effort from her.

Moving stiffly, feeling exhausted, Serena got out of bed and moved cautiously across the room to her closet, trying to avoid the shards of glass sprinkled over the rugs and the polished wood floor. There were extra lightbulbs on the closet shelf, and she took one to replace the one from her nightstand lamp. It was difficult to unscrew the burst bulb, but she managed; she didn't trust herself to flick all the shattered pieces out of existence with her powers, not when she'd come so close to losing control entirely.

When the lamp was burning again, she got a broom and dustpan and cleaned up all the bits of glass. A slow survey of the room revealed what else she had destroyed, and she shivered a little at the evidence of just how dangerous unfocused power could be.

Ironically, she couldn't repair what she had wrecked, not by using the powers that had destroyed. Because she didn't understand the technology of television or radio or even clocks, it simply wasn't possible for her to focus her powers to fix what was broken. It would be like the blind trying to put together by touch alone something they couldn't even recognize enough to define.

To create or control anything, it was first necessary to understand its very elements, its basic structure, and how it functioned. How many times had Merlin told her that? Twenty times? A hundred?

Serena sat down on her bed, still feeling drained. But not numb; that mercy wasn't granted to her. The switch she had found to contain her energies could do nothing to erase the memory of Richard with another woman.

It hurt. She couldn't believe how much it hurt. All these years she had convinced herself that she was the only woman in his life who mattered, and now she knew that wasn't true. He didn't belong only to her. He didn't belong to her at all. He really didn't see her as a woman—or, if he did, she obviously held absolutely no attraction for him.

The pain was worse, knowing that.

Dawn had lightened the windows by the time Serena tried to go back to sleep. But she couldn't. She lay beneath the covers staring up at the ceiling, feeling older than she had ever felt before. There was no limbo now, no sense of being suspended between woman and child; Serena knew she could never again be a child, not even to protect herself.

The question was—how was that going to alter her relationship with Merlin? Could she pretend there was nothing different? No. Could she even bear to look at him without crying out her pain and rage? Probably not. How would he react when she made her feelings plain, with disgust or pity? That was certainly possible. Would her raw emotion drive him even farther away from her? Or was he, even now, planning to banish her from his life completely?

Because he knew. He knew what she had discovered in the dark watches of the night.

Just before her own shock had wrenched her free of his mind, Serena had felt for a split-second *his* shock as he sensed and recognized her presence intruding on that intensely private act.

He knew. He knew she had been there.

It was another part of her pain, the discomfiting guilt and

shame of having been, however unintentionally, a voyeur. She had a memory now that she would never forget, but it was his, not hers. She'd stolen it from him . . . . And of all the things they both had to face when he came home, that one was likely to be the most difficult of all.

The only certainty Serena could find in any of it was the knowledge that nothing would ever be the same again.

SILVER FLAME
by Susan Johnson

On Sale in May

She was driven by love to break every rule . . . . Empress Jordan had fled to the Montana wilderness to escape a cruel injustice, only to find herself forced to desperate means to feed her brothers and sisters. Once she agreed to sell her most precious possession to the highest bidder, she feared she'd made a terrible mistake—even as she found herself hoping it was the tall, dark, chiseled stranger who had taken her dare and claimed her . . . .

Empress stood before him, unabashed in her nudity, and raising her emerald eyes the required height to meet his so far above, she said "What *will* you do with me, Mr. Braddock-Black?"

"Trey," he ordered, unconscious of his lightly commanding tone.

"What *will* you do with me, Trey?" she repeated correcting herself as ordered. But there was more than a hint of impudence in her tone and in her tilted mouth and arched brow.

Responding to the impudence with some of his own, he replied with a small smile, "Whatever you prefer, Empress, darling." He towered over her, clothed and booted, as dark as Lucifer, and she was intensely aware of his power and size, as if his presence seemed to invade her. "You set the pace, sweetheart," he said encouragingly, reaching out to slide the pad of one finger slowly across her shoulder. "But take your time," he went on, recognizing his own excitement, running his warm palm up her neck and cupping the back of her head lightly. Trey's voice had dropped half an octave. "We've three weeks. . . ." And for the first time in his life he looked forward to three undiluted weeks of one woman's company. It was like scenting one's mate, primordial and reflexive, and while his intellect ignored the peremptory, inexplicable compulsion, his body and blood and dragooned sensory receptors willingly complied to the urgency.

Bending his head low, his lips touched hers lightly, brushing twice across them like silken warmth before he gently slid over her mouth with his tongue and sent a shocking trail of fire curling deep down inside her.

She drew back in an unconscious response, but he'd felt the heated flame, too, and from the startled look in his eyes she knew the spark had touched them both. Trey's breathing quickened, his hand tightened abruptly on the back of her head, pulling her closer with insistence, with authority, while his other hand slid down her back until it rested warmly at the base of her spine. And when his mouth covered hers a second time, intense suddenly, more demanding, she could feel him rising hard against her. She may have been an innocent in the ways of a man and a woman, but Empress knew how animals mated in nature, and for the first time she sensed a soft warmth stirring within herself.

It was at once strange and blissful, and for a brief detached moment she felt very grown, as if a riddle of the universe were suddenly revealed. One doesn't have to love a man to feel the fire, she thought. It was at odds with all her mother had told her. Inexplicably she experienced an overwhelming sense of discovery, as if she alone knew a fundamental principle of humanity. But then her transient musing was abruptly arrested, for under the light pressure of Trey's lips she found hers opening, and the velvety, heated caress of Trey's tongue slowly entered her mouth, exploring languidly, licking her sweetness, and the heady, brandy taste of him was like a fresh treasure to be savored. She tentatively responded like a lambkin to new, unsteady legs, and when her tongue brushed his and did her own unhurried tasting, she heard him groan low in his throat. Swaying gently against her, his hard length pressed more adamantly into her yielding softness. Fire raced downward to a tingling place deep inside her as Trey's strong, insistent arousal throbbed against the soft curve of her stomach. He held her captive with his large hand low on her back as they kissed, and she felt a leaping flame speed along untried nerve endings, creating delicious new sensations. There was strange pleasure in the feel of his soft wool shirt; a melting warmth seeped through her senses, and she swayed closer into the strong male body, as if she knew instinctively that he would rarefy the enchantment. A moment later, as her mouth opened pliantly beneath his, her hands came up of their own accord and, rich with promise, rested lightly on his shoulders.

Her artless naîveté was setting his blood dangerously afire. He gave her high marks for subtlety. First the tentative withdrawal, and now the ingenuous response, was more erotic than any flagrant vice of the most skilled lover. And yet it surely must be some kind of drama, effective like the scene downstairs, where she withheld more than she offered in the concealing men's clothes and made every man in the room want to undress her.

Whether artifice, pretext, sham, or entreating supplication, the soft, imploring body melting into his, the small appealing hands warm on his shoulders, made delay suddenly inconvenient. "I think, sweet Empress," he said, his breath warm on her mouth, "*next* time you can set the pace. . . ."

Bending quickly, he lifted her into his arms and carried her to the bed. Laying her down on the rose velvet coverlet, he stood briefly and looked at her. Wanton as a Circe nymph, she looked back at him, her glance direct into his heated gaze, and she saw the smoldering, iridescent desire in his eyes. She was golden pearl juxtaposed to blush velvet, and when she slowly lifted her arms to him, he, no longer in control of himself, not detached or casual or playful as he usually was making love, took a deep breath, swiftly moved the half step to the bed, and lowered his body over hers, reaching for the buttons on his trousers with trembling fingers. His boots crushed the fine velvet but he didn't notice; she whimpered slightly when his heavy gold belt buckle pressed into her silken skin, but he kissed her in apology, intent on burying himself in the devastating Miss Jordan's lushly carnal body. His wool-clad legs pushed her pale thighs apart, and all he could think of was the feel of her closing around him. He surged forward, and she cried out softly. Maddened with desire, he thrust forward again. This time he *heard* her cry. "Oh, Christ," he breathed, urgent need suffocating in his lungs, "you can't be a virgin." He never bothered with virgins. It had been years since he'd slept with one. Lord, he was hard.

"It doesn't matter," she replied quickly, tense beneath him.

"It doesn't matter," he repeated softly, blood drumming in his temples and in his fingertips and in the soles of his feet inside the custom-made boots, and most of all in his rigid erection, insistent like a battering ram a hair's breadth from where he wanted to be so badly, he could taste the blood in his mouth. It doesn't matter, his conscience repeated. She said it doesn't matter, so it doesn't matter, and he drove in again.

Her muffled cry exploded across his lips as his mouth lowered to kiss her.

"Oh, hell." He exhaled deeply, drawing back, and, poised on his elbows, looked down at her uncertainly, his long dark hair framing his face like black silk.

"I won't cry out again," she whispered, her voice more certain than the poignant depths of her shadowy eyes. "Please . . . I must have the money."

It was all too odd and too sudden and too out of character for him. Damn . . . plundering a virgin, making her cry in fear and pain. *Steady, you'll live if you don't have her*, he told himself, but quivering need played devil's advocate to that platitude. She was urging him on. His body was even more fiercely demanding he take her. "Hell and damnation," he muttered disgruntedly. The problem was terrible, demanding immediate answers, and he wasn't thinking too clearly, only feeling a delirious excitement quite detached from moral judgment. And adamant. "Bloody hell," he breathed, and in that moment, rational thought gained a fingertip control on the ragged edges of his lust. "Keep the money. I don't want to—" He said it quickly, before he'd change his mind, then paused and smiled. "Obviously that's not entirely true, but I don't ruin virgins," he said levelly.

Empress had not survived the death of her parents and the months following, struggling to stay alive in the wilderness, without discovering in herself immense strength. She summoned it now, shakily but determinedly. "It's not a moral dilemma. It's a business matter and my responsibility. I insist."

He laughed, his smile close and deliciously warm. "Here I'm refusing a woman insisting I take her virginity. I must be crazy."

"The world's crazy sometimes, I think," she replied softly, aware of the complex reasons prompting her conduct.

"Tonight, at least," he murmured, "it's more off track than usual." But even for a wild young man notorious as a womanizer, the offered innocence was too strangely bizarre. And maybe too businesslike for a man who found pleasure and delight in the act. It was not flattering to be a surrogate for a business matter. "Look," he said with an obvious effort, "thanks but no thanks. I'm not interested. But keep the money. I admire your courage." And rolling off her, he lay on his back and shouted, "*Flo!*"

"No!" Empress cried, and was on top of him before he drew his next breath, terrified he'd change his mind about the money, terrified he'd change his mind in the morning when his head was clear and he woke up in Flo's arms. Fifty thousand dollars was a huge sum of money to give away on a whim, or to lose to some misplaced moral scruple. She must convince him to stay with her, then at least she could earn the money. Or at least try.

Lying like silken enchantment on his lean, muscled body, she covered his face with kisses. Breathless, rushing kisses, a young girls's simple closemouthed kisses. Then, in a flush of boldness, driven by necessity, a tentative dancing lick of her small tongue slid down his straight nose, to his waiting mouth. When her tongue lightly caressed the arched curve of his upper lip, his hands came up and closed on her naked shoulders, and he drew the teasing tip into his mouth. He sucked on it gently, slowly, as if he envisioned a lifetime without interruptions, until the small, sun-kissed shoulders beneath his hands trembled in tiny quivers.

Strange, fluttering wing beats sped through her heating blood, and a curious languor caused Empress to twine her arms around Trey's strong neck. But her heart was beating hard like the Indian drums whose sound carried far up to their hidden valley in summer, for fear outweighed languor still. He mustn't go to Flo. Slipping her fingers through the black luster of his long hair, ruffled in loose waves on his neck, she brushed her mouth along his cheek. "Please," she whispered near his ear, visions of her hope to save her family dashed by his reluctance, "stay with me." It was a simple plea, simply put. It was perhaps her last chance. Her lips traced the perfect curve of his ears, and his hands tightened their grip in response. "Say it's all right. Say I can stay. . . ." She was murmuring rapidly in a flurry of words.

How should he answer the half-shy, quicksilver words? Why was she insisting? Why did the flattery of a woman wanting him matter?

Then she shifted a little so her leg slid between his, a sensual, instinctive movement, and the smooth velvet of his masculinity rose against her thigh. It was warm, it was hot, and like a child might explore a new sensation, she moved her leg lazily up its length.

Trey's mouth went dry, and he couldn't convince himself that refusal was important any longer. He groaned, thinking, there are some things in life without answers. His hand was trembling when he drew her mouth back to his.

A moment later, when Flo knocked and called out his name, Empress shouted, "Go away!" And when Flo repeated his name, Trey's voice carried clearly through the closed door. "I'll be down later."

He was rigid but tense and undecided, and Empress counted on the little she knew about masculine desire to accomplish what her logical explanation hadn't. Being French, she was well aware that *amour* could be heated and fraught with urgent emotion, but she was unsure exactly about the degree of urgency relative to desire.

But she knew what had happened moments before when she'd tasted his mouth and recalled how he'd responded to her yielding softness, so she practiced her limited expertise with a determined persistence. She must be sure she had the money. And if it would assure her family their future, her virginity was paltry stuff in the bargain.

"Now let's begin again," she whispered.

THE MAGNIFICENT ROGUE
by Iris Johansen

On Sale in August

From the glittering court of Queen Elizabeth to the barren island of Craighdu, THE MAGNIFICENT ROGUE is the spellbinding story of courageous love and unspeakable evil. The daring chieftain of a Scottish clan, Robert MacDarren knows no fear, and only the threat to a kinsman's life makes him bow to Queen Elizabeth's order that he wed Kathryn Ann Kentrye. He's aware of the dangerous secret in Kate's past, a secret that could destroy a great empire, but he doesn't expect the stirring of desire when he first lays eyes on the fragile beauty. Grateful to escape the tyranny of her guardian, Kate accepts the mesmerizing stranger as her husband. But even as they discover a passion greater than either has known, enemies are weaving their poisonous web around them, and soon Robert and Kate must risk their very lives to defy the ultimate treachery.

In the following scene, Robert and his cousin Gavin Gordon have come to Kate's home to claim her—and she flees.

She was being followed!

Sebastian?

Kate paused a moment on the trail and caught a glimpse of dark hair and the shimmer of the gold necklace about her pursuer's neck. Not Sebastian. Robert MacDarren.

The wild surge of disappointment she felt at the realization was completely unreasonable. He must have come at Sebastian's bidding, which meant her guardian had persuaded him to his way of thinking. Well, what had she expected? He was a stranger and Sebastian was a respected man of the cloth. There was no reason why he would be different from any of the others. How clever of Sebastian to send someone younger and stronger than himself to search her out, she thought bitterly.

She turned and began to run, her shoes sinking into the mud with every step. She glanced over her shoulder.

He was closer. He was not running, but his long legs covered the ground steadily, effortlessly, as his gaze studied the trail in front of him. He had evidently not seen her yet and was only following her tracks.

She was growing weaker. Her head felt peculiarly light and her breath was coming in painful gasps. She couldn't keep running.

And she couldn't surrender.

Which left only one solution to her dilemma. She sprinted several yards ahead and then darted into the underbrush at the side of the trail.

Hurry. She had to hurry. Her gaze frantically searched the underbrush. Ah, there was one.

She pounced on a heavy branch and then backtracked several yards and held it, waiting.

She must aim for the head. She had the strength for only one blow and it must drop him.

Her breath sounded heavily and terribly loud. She had to breathe more evenly or he would hear her.

He was almost upon her.

Her hands tightened on the branch.

He went past her, his expression intent as he studied the tracks.

She drew a deep breath, stepped out on the trail behind him, and swung the branch with all her strength.

He grunted in pain and then slowly crumpled to the ground.

She dropped the branch and ran past his body and darted down the trail again.

Something struck the back of her knees. She was falling!

She hit the ground so hard, the breath left her body. Blackness swirled around her.

When the darkness cleared, she realized she was on her back, her arms pinned on each side of her head. Robert MacDarren was astride her body.

She started to struggle.

"Lie still, dammit." His hands tightened cruelly on her arms. "I'm not—Ouch!"

She had turned her head and sunk her teeth into his wrist. She could taste the coppery flavor of blood in her mouth, but his grip didn't ease.

"Let me go!" How stupidly futile the words were when she knew he had no intention of releasing her.

She tried to butt her head against his chest, but she couldn't reach him.

"Really, Robert, can't you wait until the words are said for you to climb on top of her?" Gavin Gordon said from behind MacDarren.

"It's about time you got here," MacDarren said in a growl. "She's trying to kill me."

'Aye, for someone who couldn't lift her head, she's doing quite well. I saw her strike the blow." Gavin grinned. "But I was too far away to come to your rescue. Did she do any damage?"

"I'm going to have one hell of a headache."

Kate tried to knee him in the groin, but he quickly moved upward on her body.

"Your hand's bleeding," Gavin observed.

"She's taken a piece out of me. I can see why Landfield kept the ropes on her."

The ropes. Despair tore through her as she realized how completely Sebastian had won him to his way of thinking. The man would bind her and take her back to Sebastian. She couldn't fight against both MacDarren and Gordon and would use the last of her precious strength trying to do so. She would have to wait for a better opportunity to present itself. She stopped fighting and lay there staring defiantly at him.

"Very sensible," MacDarren said grimly. "I'm not in a very good temper at the moment. I don't think you want to make it worse."

"Get off me."

"And have you run away again?" MacDarren shook his head. "You've caused me enough trouble for one day. Give me your belt, Gavin."

Gavin took off his wide leather belt and handed it to MacDarren, who buckled the belt about her wrists and drew it tight.

"I'm not going back to the cottage," she said with the fierceness born of desperation. "I *can't* go back there."

He got off her and rose to his feet. "You'll go where I tell you to go, even if I have to drag—" He stopped in self-disgust as he realized what he had said. "Christ, I sound like that bastard." The anger suddenly left him as he looked at her lying there before him. "You're afraid of him?"

Fear was always with her when she thought of Sebastian, but she would not admit it. She sat up and repeated, "I can't go back."

He studied her for a moment. "All right, we won't go back. You'll never have to see him again."

She stared at him in disbelief.

He turned to Gavin. "We'll stay the night at that inn we passed at the edge of the village. Go back to the cottage and get her belongings and then saddle the horses. We'll meet you at the stable."

Gavin nodded and the next moment disappeared into the underbrush.

MacDarren glanced down at Kate. "I trust you don't object to that arrangement?"

She couldn't comprehend his words. "You're taking me away?"

"If you'd waited, instead of jumping out the window, I would have told you that two hours ago. That's why I came."

Then she thought she understood. "You're taking me to the lady?"

He shook his head. "It appears Her Majesty thinks it's time you wed."

Shock upon shock. "Wed?"

He said impatiently, "You say that as if you don't know what it means. You must have had instructions on the duties of wifehood."

"I know what it means." Slavery and suffocation and cruelty. From what she could judge from Sebastian and Martha's marriage, a wife's lot was little better than her own. True, he did not beat Martha, but the screams she heard from their bedroom while they mated had filled her with sick horror. But she had thought she would never have to worry about that kind of mistreatment. "I can never marry."

"Is that what the good vicar told you?" His lips tightened. "Well, it appears the queen disagrees."

Then it might come to pass. Even Sebastian obeyed the queen. The faintest hope began to spring within her. Even though marriage was only another form of slavery, perhaps the queen had chosen an easier master than Sebastian for her. "Who am I to marry?"

He smiled sardonically. "I have that honor."

Another shock and not a pleasant one. Easy was not a term anyone would use to describe this man. She blurted, "And you're not afraid?"

"Afraid of you? Not if I have someone to guard my back."

That wasn't what she meant, but of course he wouldn't be afraid. She doubted if he feared anything or anyone, and, besides, she wasn't what Sebastian said she was. He had said the words so often, she sometimes found herself believing him, and she was so tired now, she wasn't thinking clearly. The strength was seeping out of her with every passing second. "No, you shouldn't be afraid." She swayed. "Not Lilith . . ."

"More like a muddy gopher," he muttered as he reached out and steadied her. "We have to get to the stable. Can you walk, or shall I carry you?"

"I can walk." She dismissed the outlandish thought of marriage from her mind. She would ponder the implications of this change in her life later. There were more important matters to consider now. "But we have to get Caird."

"Caird? Who the devil is Caird?"

"My horse." She turned and started through the underbrush. "Before we go I have to fetch him. He's not far. . . ."

She could hear the brush shift and whisper as he followed her. "Your horse is in the forest?"

"I was hiding him from Sebastian. He was going to kill him. He wanted me to tell him where he was."

"And that was why he was dragging you?"

She ignored the question. "Sebastian said the forest beasts would devour him. He frightened me." She was staggering with exhaustion, but she couldn't give up now. "It's been such a while since I left him." She rounded a corner of a trail and breathed a sigh of relief as she caught sight of Caird calmly munching grass under the shelter of an oak tree. "No, he's fine."

"You think so?" MacDarren's skeptical gaze raked the piebald stallion from its swayback to its knobby knees. "I see nothing fine about him. How old is he?"

"Almost twenty." She reached the horse and tenderly began to stroke his muzzle. "But he's strong and very good-tempered."

"He won't do," MacDarren said flatly. "We'll have to get rid of him. He'd never get through the Highlands. We'll leave him with the innkeeper and I'll buy you another horse."

"I *won't* get rid of him," she said fiercely. "I can't just leave him. How would I know if they'd take good care of him? He goes with us."

"And I say he stays."

The words were spoken with such absolute resolution that they sent a jolt of terror through her. They reminded her of Sebastian's edicts, from which there was no appeal. She moistened her lips. "Then I'll have to stay too."

MacDarren's gaze narrowed on her face. "And what if Landfield catches you again?"

She shrugged and leaned her cheek wearily against Caird's muzzle. "He belongs to me," she said simply.

She could feel his gaze on her back and sensed his exasperation. "Oh, for God's sake!" He picked up her saddle from the ground by the tree and threw it on Caird's back. He began to buckle the cinches. "All right, we'll take him."

Joy soared through her. "Truly?"

"I said it, didn't I?" He picked her up and tossed her into the saddle. "We'll use him as a pack horse and I'll get you another mount to ride. Satisfied?"

Satisfied! She smiled brilliantly. "Oh yes. You won't regret it. But you needn't spend your money on another horse. Caird is really very strong. I'm sure he'll be able to—"

"I'm already regretting it." His tone was distinctly edgy as he began to lead the horse through the forest. "Even carrying a light load, I doubt if he'll get through the Highlands."

It was the second time he had mentioned these forbidding Highlands, but she didn't care where they were going as long as they were taking Caird. "But you'll do it? You won't change your mind?"

For an instant his expression softened as he saw the eagerness in her face. "I won't change my mind."

Gavin was already mounted and waiting when they arrived at the stable a short time later. A grin lit his face as he glanced from Kate to the horse and then back again. "Hers?"

Robert nodded. "And the cause of all this turmoil."

"A fitting pair," Gavin murmured. "She has a chance of cleaning up decently, but the horse . . ." He shook his head. "No hope for it, Robert."

"My thought exactly. But we're keeping him anyway."

Gavin's brows lifted. "Oh, are we? Interesting . . ."

Robert swung into the saddle. "Any trouble with the vicar and his wife?"

Kate's hands tensed on the reins.

"Mistress Landfield appeared to be overjoyed to give me the girl's belongings." He nodded at a small bundle tied to the saddle. "And the vicar just glowered at me."

"Perhaps he's given up."

"He won't give up," Kate whispered. "He never gives up."

"Then perhaps we'd better go before we encounter him again," Robert said as he kicked his horse into a trot. "Keep an eye on her, Gavin. She's almost reeling in that saddle."

Sebastian was waiting for them a short distance from the cottage. He stood blocking the middle of the path.

"Get out of the way," Robert said coldly. "I'm not in the mood for this."

"It's your last chance," Sebastian said. "Give her back to me before it's too late."

"Stand aside, Landfield."

"Kathryn." Sebastian turned to her and his voice was pleading. "Do not go. You know you can never wed. You know what will happen."

Robert rode forward and his horse's shoulder forced Sebastian to the side of the trail. He motioned Gavin and Kate to ride ahead. "It's over. She's no longer your responsibility." His voice lowered to soft deadliness. "And if you ever approach her again, I'll make sure I never see you repeat the mistake."

"You'll see me." Landfield's eyes shimmered with tears as his gaze clung to Kate. "I wanted to spare you, Kathryn. I wanted to save you, but God has willed otherwise. You know what has to be done now."

He turned and walked heavily back toward the cottage.

"What did he mean?" Gavin asked as his curious gaze followed Landfield.

She didn't answer as she watched Sebastian stalk away. She realized she was shivering with a sense of impending doom. How foolish. This was what he wanted her to feel, his way of chaining her to him.

"Well?" Robert asked.

"Nothing. He just wanted to make me afraid." She moistened her lips. "He likes me to be afraid of him."

She could see he didn't believe her and thought he would pursue it. Instead he said quietly, "You don't have to fear him any longer. He no longer holds any power over you." He held her gaze with a mesmerizing power. "I'm the only one who does now."

OFFICIAL RULES TO WINNERS CLASSIC SWEEPSTAKES

No Purchase necessary. To enter the sweepstakes follow instructions found elsewhere in this offer. You can also enter the sweepstakes by hand printing your name, address, city, state and zip code on a 3" x 5" piece of paper and mailing it to: Winners Classic Sweepstakes, P.O. Box 785, Gibbstown, NJ 08027. Mail each entry separately. Sweepstakes begins 12/1/91. Entries must be received by 6/1/93. Some presentations of this sweepstakes may feature a deadline for the Early Bird prize. If the offer you receive does, then to be eligible for the Early Bird prize your entry must be received according to the Early Bird date specified. Not responsible for lost, late, damaged, misdirected, illegible or postage due mail. Mechanically reproduced entries are not eligible. All entries become property of the sponsor and will not be returned.

Prize Selection/Validations: Winners will be selected in random drawings on or about 7/30/93, by VENTURA ASSOCIATES, INC., an independent judging organization whose decisions are final. Odds of winning are determined by total number of entries received. Circulation of this sweepstakes is estimated not to exceed 200 million. Entrants need not be present to win. All prizes are guaranteed to be awarded and delivered to winners. Winners will be notified by mail and may be required to complete an affidavit of eligibility and release of liability which must be returned within 14 days of date of notification or alternate winners will be selected. Any guest of a trip winner will also be required to execute a release of liability. Any prize notification letter or any prize returned to a participating sponsor, Bantam Doubleday Dell Publishing Group, Inc., its participating divisions or subsidiaries, or VENTURA ASSOCIATES, INC. as undeliverable will be awarded to an alternate winner. Prizes are not transferable. No multiple prize winners except as may be necessary due to unavailability, in which case a prize of equal or greater value will be awarded. Prizes will be awarded approximately 90 days after the drawing. All taxes, automobile license and registration fees, if applicable, are the sole responsibility of the winners. Entry constitutes permission (except where prohibited) to use winners' names and likenesses for publicity purposes without further or other compensation.

Participation: This sweepstakes is open to residents of the United States and Canada, except for the province of Quebec. This sweepstakes is sponsored by Bantam Doubleday Dell Publishing Group, Inc. (BDD), 666 Fifth Avenue, New York, NY 10103. Versions of this sweepstakes with different graphics will be offered in conjunction with various solicitations or promotions by different subsidiaries and divisions of BDD. Employees and their families of BDD, its division, subsidiaries, advertising agencies, and VENTURA ASSOCIATES, INC., are not eligible.

Canadian residents, in order to win, must first correctly answer a time limited arithmetical skill testing question. Void in Quebec and wherever prohibited or restricted by law. Subject to all federal, state, local and provincial laws and regulations.

Prizes: The following values for prizes are determined by the manufacturers' suggested retail prices or by what these items are currently known to be selling for at the time this offer was published. Approximate retail values include handling and delivery of prizes. Estimated maximum retail value of prizes: 1 Grand Prize ($27,500 if merchandise or $25,000 Cash); 1 First Prize ($3,000); 5 Second Prizes ($400 each); 35 Third Prizes ($100 each); 1,000 Fourth Prizes ($9.00 each) ; 1 Early Bird Prize ($5,000); Total approximate maximum retail value is $50,000. Winners will have the option of selecting any prize offered at level won. Automobile winner must have a valid driver's license at the time the car is awarded. Trips are subject to space and departure availability. Certain black-out dates may apply. Travel must be completed within one year from the time the prize is awarded. Minors must be accompanied by an adult. Prizes won by minors will be awarded in the name of parent or legal guardian.

For a list of Major Prize Winners (available after 7/30/93): send a self-addressed, stamped envelope entirely separate from your entry to: Winners Classic Sweepstakes Winners, P.O. Box 825, Gibbstown, NJ 08027. Requests must be received by 6/1/93. DO NOT SEND ANY OTHER CORRESPONDENCE TO THIS P.O. BOX.

SWP 9/92

Don't miss these fabulous Bantam women's fiction titles on sale in May

SACRED LIES

☐ 29063-0 $5.99/6.99 in Canada

by Dianne Edouard & Sandra Ware

Authors of MORTAL SINS

A beautiful agent is drawn into a web of betrayal and desire—where she must choose between who to believe…and who to love.

THE WIZARD OF SEATTLE

☐ 28999-3 $5.50/6.50 in Canada

by Kay Hooper

Co-author of THE DELANEY CHRISTMAS CAROL

A magical romantic fantasy!
From Seattle to Ancient Atlantis, Richard Patrick Merlin and Serena Smyth struggle for control of her spectacular gift of magic—defying a taboo so ancient that the reasons for its existence have been forgotten—risking all for an eternal love.

SILVER FLAME

☐ 29959-X $5.50/6.50 in Canada

by Susan Johnson

Bestselling author of SINFUL and FORBIDDEN

The Braddock-Black dynasty continues!
The fires of romance are white hot when Empress Jordan flees to the Montana wilderness…and finds a man as wild as the land around him.

Ask for these books at your local bookstore or use this page to order.

☐ Please send me the books I have checked above. I am enclosing $ _____ (add $2.50 to cover postage and handling). Send check or money order, no cash or C. O. D.'s please.

Name _____

Address _____

City/ State/ Zip _____

Send order to: Bantam Books, Dept. FN104, 2451 S. Wolf Rd., Des Plaines, IL 60018
Allow four to six weeks for delivery.
Prices and availability subject to change without notice.

FN104 6/93

Don't miss these fabulous Bantam women's fiction titles on sale in June

☐
LADY VALIANT
29575-6 $5.50/6.50 in Canada
by Suzanne Robinson

Bestselling author of LADY DEFIANT

"An author with star quality....Spectacularly talented."
—*Romantic Times*

*Once Mary, Queen of Scots, had been her closest friend.
Now Thea Hunt was determined to pay back the queen's
kindness—by journeying to Scotland to warn her away from
a treacherous marriage. But in the thick of an English forest,
Thea suddenly finds herself set upon by thieves...and
chased down by a golden-haired highwayman who'd still her
struggles—and stir her heart—with one penetrating glance
from his fiery blue eyes.*

☐
MASK OF NIGHT
29062-2 $4.99/5.99/6.50 in Canada
by Lois Wolfe

Author of THE SCHEMERS

*"Fast paced, highly evocative, filled with action, surprises,
and shocking revelations....an intriguing, different Civil War
romance."* —*Romantic Times* on *The Schemers*

*In St. Louis in the late 1800s, a fair-haired beauty and a
bankrupt cattleman hell-bent on revenge are drawn to each
other across the footlights...but the heat of their passion
would ignite a fire that could burn them both.*

Ask for these books at your local bookstore or use this page to order.

❏ Please send me the books I have checked above. I am enclosing $ _____ (add $2.50
to cover postage and handling). Send check or money order, no cash or C. O. D.'s please.

Name _____

Address _____

City/ State/ Zip _____

Send order to: Bantam Books, Dept. FN105, 2451 S. Wolf Rd., Des Plaines, IL 60018
Allow four to six weeks for delivery.

Prices and availability subject to change without notice.   FN105 6/93

The Very Best In Contemporary Women's Fiction

Sandra Brown

_____ 29085-1 22 INDIGO PLACE .... $4.50/5.50 in Canada
_____ 56045-X TEMPERATURES RISING $5.99/6.99
_____ 28990-X TEXAS! CHASE $5.99/6.99
_____ 28951-9 TEXAS! LUCKY $5.99/6.99
_____ 29500-4 TEXAS! SAGE $5.99/6.99
_____ 29783-X A WHOLE NEW LIGHT $5.99/6.99

Tami Hoag

_____ 29534-9 LUCKY'S LADY $4.99/5.99
_____ 29053-3 MAGIC $4.99/5.99
_____ 29272-2 STILL WATERS $4.99/5.99
_____ 56050-6 SARAH'S SIN $4.50/5.50

Nora Roberts

_____ 27283-7 BRAZEN VIRTUE $4.99/5.99
_____ 29597-7 CARNAL INNOCENCE $5.50/6.50
_____ 29490-3 DIVINE EVIL $5.99/6.99
_____ 29078-9 GENUINE LIES $4.99/5.99
_____ 26461-3 HOT ICE $4.99/5.99
_____ 28578-5 PUBLIC SECRETS $4.95/5.95
_____ 26574-1 SACRED SINS $5.50/6.50
_____ 27859-2 SWEET REVENGE $5.50/6.50

Pamela Simpson

_____ 29424-5 FORTUNE'S CHILD $5.99/6.99

Deborah Smith

_____ 29690-6 BLUE WILLOW $5.50/6.50
_____ 29092-4 FOLLOW THE SUN $4.99/5.99
_____ 29107-6 MIRACLE $4.50/5.50

Ask for these titles at your bookstore or use this page to order.

Please send me the books I have checked above. I am enclosing $ _____ (add $2.50 to
cover postage and handling). Send check or money order, no cash or C. O. D.'s please.

Mr./ Ms. _____

Address _____

City/ State/ Zip _____

Send order to: Bantam Books, Dept. FN24, 2451 S. Wolf Road, Des Plaines, IL 60018
Please allow four to six weeks for delivery.

Prices and availability subject to change without notice.   FN 24 - 3/93